VIRGIN WHOLLY MARVELOUS

Praises of Our Lady from the Popes, Councils, Saints, and Doctors of the Church

Virgin wholly marvelous
   Who didst bear God's Son for us,
Who can praise thee as he ought
   Gifts with every blessing fraught,
Gifts that bring the holy life,
Thou didst grant us Maiden-Wife.

St. Ephraem +373

Tr. J. W. Atkinson, S.J. (+1921)

Virgin Wholly Marvelous

Praises of Our Lady by the Popes, Councils, Saints, and Doctors of the Church

Edited by
David Supple, O.S.B.

THE RAVENGATE PRESS
Cambridge

1999 Edition

Imprimi Potest

+ Raphael De Salvo, O.S.B.
Abbot President,
Swiss-American Federation
of the Order of St. Benedict

Imprimatur

+ Bernard J. Flanagan
Bishop of Worcester

July 20, 1981

The *Imprimatur* is an official declaration that a book or pamphlet is free of doctrinal and moral error. No implication is contained therein that the authority granting the *Imprimatur* agrees with the contents, opinions or statements expressed.

Please address orders and inquiries to:
The Ravengate Press
Post Office Box 49
Still River, Massachusetts 01467-0049

LIBRARY OF CONGRESS CATALOGING IN PUBLICATION DATA

Virgin Wholly Marvelous

1. Mary, Blessed Virgin, Saint—Meditations.
I. Supple, David, 1919–1982.
BT602.V55   232.91   81-13928

ISBN 0-911218-18-1
ISBN 0-911218-17-3 (pbk.)   81-13928
                                                                 AACR2

PRINTED IN THE UNITED STATES OF AMERICA

for
L.F.

INTRODUCTION

Was there ever a creature that the Trinity dealt more intimately with than Our Blessed Lady? Daughter of the Father, Mother of the Son, and Spouse of the Holy Spirit, she is the route God took to make His Son incarnate. She it is who "leaves His light sifted to suit our sight"* and for that makes Christians ever after anxious to pay her honour.

VIRGIN WHOLLY MARVELOUS is a collection of short quotations from the Popes, Councils, Saints, and Doctors of the Church in praise of Our Lady.

All the quotations included herein are from the public domain of the documents of history. It would, however, be grossly negligent of the complier not to acknowledge his indebtedness to Benjamin Musser's *Florilegium Mariae*, a much vaster work, which was printed privately in a limited edition by the author in thanksgiving for his conversion to Catholicism.

Still River   D.S.

1981

*G.M. Hopkins +1889

ABBREVIATIONS

Ab.	Abbot
Abp.	Archbishop
Bp	Bishop
BVM	Blessed Virgin Mary
C.	Confessor
Cist.	Cistercian (Order of Citeaux)
C.P.	Congregation of the Passion (Passionists)
C.SS.R.	Congregation of the Most Holy Redeemer
M.	Martyr (Redemptorists)
O. Carm.	Order of Mount Carmel (Carmelites)
O.F.M.	Order of Friars Minor (Franciscans)
O.F.M. Cap.	Order of Friars Minor Capuchin (Capuchins)
O.P.	Order of Preachers (Dominicans)
O.S.A.	Order of St. Augustine (Augustinians)
O.S.B.	Order of St. Benedict (Benedictines)
Pr.	Priest
S.J.	Society of Jesus (Jesuits)
V.	Virgin

Contents

VIRGIN WHOLLY MARVELOUS

Praises of Our Lady from the Popes, Councils, Saints, and Doctors of the Church

I

The Virgin Birth

1. The same eternal Only-begotten Son of the eternal Father was born of the Holy Spirit and the Virgin Mary . . . . That is to say, He was conceived of the Holy Spirit in the womb of His Virgin Mother who brought Him forth without detriment to her virginity, as, too, she had, without detriment to her virginity, conceived Him.

—*Pope St. Leo the Great*
Doctor of the Church (+461)

2. As the Angel Gabriel had declared to her, the Holy Spirit overshadowed her, hence, while remaining a virgin, she became the Mother of the Word of God, Who took flesh of her.

—*Catechism of Pope St. Pius X* (+1914)

3. If anyone does not, according to the Holy Fathers, and according to the truth of God, confess that the ever-Virgin and Immaculate Mary, the Mother of God, conceived in time, truly and in special manner, without seed, of the Holy Spirit, the Very Word of God, Who was born of all ages of God the Father, and that she begot Him without corruption, remaining a virgin after her child-bearing, let him be condemned.

—*Council of Toledo, 17 November 675*

4. As Adam was born from the virgin earth, so Jesus Christ must have been born of a virgin mother.

—*St. Irenaeus, Bp. M.* (+c. 202)

5. Truly do we proclaim Mary to be both Virgin and Mother, for true fecundity glorified her virginity and undefiled virginity

glorified her true fecundity. Her virginity was rendered more glorious by her fecundity, and her fecundity by her virginity.

—*St. Augustine, Bp. C.*
Doctor of the Church (+430)

6.   He Who wrote on the tablets of stone without iron, made Mary with child of the Holy Ghost; and He Who produced bread in the desert without ploughing, impregnated the Virgin without corruption; and He Who made the rod to bud without rain, made the daughter of David bring forth without seed.

—*St. Augustine, Bp. C.*
Doctor of the Church (+430)

7.   A Virgin Mother was chosen, who would conceive without concupiscence, and who brought forth a Man without a man.

—*St. Augustine, Bp. C.*
Doctor of the Church (+430)

8.   Truly are you blessed among women, who without example to womankind rejoice in the honor of a mother and the beauty of virginity, and as becomes a virgin-mother, you have given life to the Son of God.

—*St. Bede the Venerable, O.S.B.*
Doctor of the Church (+735)

9.   Christ is born of a woman, but one to whom the fruit of fecundity came in such a manner that the flower of virginity did not fall.

—*St. Bernard of Clairvaux, Cist.*
Doctor of the Church (+1153)

10. A ray from the star does not diminish its brightness, neither does the Son of the Virgin lessen the virginity of His Mother.

—*St. Bernard of Clairvaux, Cist.*
Doctor of the Church (+1153)

11. She was chaste in her virginal body, as the Evangelist testifies, saying: *And the name of the Virgin was Mary* (Luke 1:27).
In her virginal mind Mary was even more chaste, as she herself
testifies. For she said to the Angel: *How shall this be done, for I
know not man* (Luke 1:34). That is to say, I do not intend to
know a man.

—*St. Bonaventure, O.F.M., Bp. C.*
Doctor of the Church (+1274)

12. St. Gregory of Nyssa (+c. 395) says, that so much did the
Blessed Virgin love this virtue (of perpetual virginity), that to
preserve it, she would have been willing to renounce even the
dignity of Mother of God. This we may conclude from her
answer to the Archangel, *How shall this be done, because I know
not man?* (Luke 1:34) and from the words she afterward added,
Be it done to me according to your word (v. 38), signifying that she
gave her consent on the condition that as the angel had assured
her, she would become a mother only by the overshadowing of
the Holy Ghost.

—*St. Alphonsus Liguori, C.SS.R., Bp. C.*
Doctor of the Church (+1787)

13. *Words of Jesus to Gertrude:* "Praise me also for the spotless
and perfect virginity of Her who conceived me as a virgin, bore
me as a virgin, and virgin remained after my birth, ever imitating
my innocence."

—*St. Gertrude the Great, O.S.B., V.* (+1301)

14. *Words of Mary to Gertrude:* "In no way should my Son be
referred to as my *only-begotten*, but rather my *first-born*, for
indeed I first gave birth to my sweetest Jesus without impair-
ment to my virginity, and then after Him, or better still, through
Him, I gave birth to you, by adopting you as his brothers and
my children, in my loving and maternal bosom."

—*St. Gertrude the Great, O.S.B., V.* (+1301)

15. On Matins of the feast of the Annunciation, I saw the heart of the Virgin Mother so bathed by the rivers of grace flowing out of the Blessed Trinity, that I understood the privilege Mary has of being the *most powerful* after God the Father, the *wisest* after God the Son, and the *most benign* after God the Holy Spirit.

—*St. Gertrude the Great, O.S.B., V.* (+*1301*)

16. I believe that Mary was both virgin and mother: I believe that she was a virgin before giving birth; I believe that she was a virgin while giving birth; I believe that she was a virgin after giving birth; and this doctrine which I believe, I love, because it was done for love of me.

—*St. Ildephonsus, Bp. C.* (+*667*)

17. Both Mary's virginity and her giving birth to Jesus, were kept hidden from the prince of this world.

—*St. Ignatius of Antioch, Bp. M.* (+*107*)

18. The belief in the Virgin birth has been handed over to the Church by the Apostles and by their disciples, the same as the other truths of the Faith.

—*St. Irenaeus, Bp. M.* (+*c. 202*)

II

Holy Nativity of Mary

1. *Who is she that cometh forth as the morning rising* (Cant. 6:9)? Yes, for as the dawn is the end of night, and the beginning of

day, well may the Blessed Virgin Mary, who was the end of vices, be called the dawn of day.

                    —*Pope Innocent III* (+1216)

2.   Come, all ye peoples! Come all, whoever or wherever you are; come and unite in celebrating the birth of the Virgin, with whom is likewise born our salvation.

                    —*St. John Damascene, Pr. C.*
                Doctor of the Church (+c. 749)

3.   *And there shall come forth a rod out of the root of Jesse, and a flower shall rise up out of his root* (Isaias 11:1). This divine Mother is that powerful rod with which the violence of the infernal enemies is conquered.

                    —*St. Peter Damian, Bp. C.*
                Doctor of the Church (+1072)

4.   *All are born children of wrath* (Eph. 2:3). Oh, how far from this woe of them that are born was the most holy Nativity of Mary, who was not only free from original sin, but also from the fuel of misery, insofar as it leads to sin, for she was conceived without stain.

                    —*St. Bonaventure, O.F.M., Bp. C.*
                Doctor of the Church (+1274)

5.   Our heavenly child, because she was appointed mediatress of the world, as also because she was destined to be the Mother of the Redeemer, received, at the very beginning of her existence, grace exceeding in greatness that of all the saints together. Hence, how delightful a sight must the beautiful soul of this happy child have been to Heaven and earth!

                    —*St. Alphonsus Liguori, C.SS.R., Bp. C.*
                Doctor of the Church (+1787)

III

Most Holy Name of Mary

1. The name of Mary is the key of the gates of Heaven.

—St. Ephraem of Edessa
Doctor of the Church (+c. 373)

2. Your name, O Mary, is a precious onintment, which breathes forth the odor of Divine grace. Let this ointment of salvation enter the inmost recesses of our souls.

—St. Ambrose, Bp. C.
Doctor of the Church (+397)

3. The name of Mary is an indication of chastity.

—St. Peter Chrysologus, Bp. C.
Doctor of the Church (+c. 450)

4. Mary means *light*, for from her proceeded Christ, the Light of the world.

—St. Isidore of Seville
Doctor of the Church (+636)

5. As breathing is not only a sign but even a cause of life, so the name of Mary, which is constantly found on the lips of God's servants, both proves that they are truly alive, and at the same time causes and preserves their life, and gives them every succor.

—St. Germanus of Constantinople, Bp. C. (+c. 732)

6. May your name, O Mother of God, be the last sound that escapes my lips.

—St. Germanus of Constantinople, Bp. C. (+c. 732)

7.   Your name, O Mother of God, is filled with divine graces and blessings.

—*St. Methodius, C.* (+847)

8.   O name of Mary! Joy in the heart, honey in the mouth, melody to the ear of her devout clients!

—*St. Anthony of Padua, O.F.M.*
Doctor of the Church (+1231)

9.   Glorious indeed, and admirable is your name, O Mary; for those who pronounce it at death need not fear all the powers of hell. . . . Men do not fear a powerful hostile army as the powers of hell fear the name and protection of Mary.

—*St. Bonaventure, O.F.M., Bp. C.*
Doctor of the Church (+1274)

10. As wax melts before fire, so do the devils lose their power against those souls who remember the name of Mary and devoutly invoke it.

—*St. Bonaventure, O.F.M., Bp. C.*
Doctor of the Church (+1274)

11. *Ave Maria!* This name was inserted (in the Angelic Salutation) not by the Angel, but by the devotion of the faithful. The blessed Evangelist Luke says significantly, *And the name of the Virgin was Mary* (Luke 1:27). This most holy, sweet and worthy name was eminently fitting to so holy, sweet and worthy a virgin. For Mary means a *bitter sea, star of the sea*, the *illuminated* or *illuminatrix*. Mary is interpreted *lady*. Mary is a bitter sea to the demons; to men she is the star of the sea; to the angels she is illuminatrix, and to all creatures she is lady. . . . Let us pray, let us pray most devoutly to Mary and say: O Mary, Bitter Sea, help us, that we may be plunged into the bitter sea of penance! O Mary, Star of the Sea, help us, that we may be guided rightly

through the sea of this world! O Mary, Light-giver, help us, that
we may be eternally illumined in glory! O Lady Mary, help us
by your government and empire that we may be filially gov-
erned. Through Our Lord Jesus Christ. Amen.

—*St. Bonaventure, O.F.M., Bp. C.*
Doctor of the Church (+1274)

12. Mary means *star of the sea*, for as mariners are guided to port
by the ocean star, so Christians attain to glory through Mary's
maternal intercession.

—*St. Thomas Aquinas, O.P., C.*
Doctor of the Church (+1274)

13. O Mary, what must you yourself be, since your very name is
so loving and gracious?

—*Blessed Henry Suso, O.P.* (+1365)

14. When I pronounce the name of Mary, I feel myself inflamed
with such love and joy, that between the tears and happiness
with which I pronounce this beautiful name, I feel as though my
heart might leave my breast! For this sweet name is like a honey-
comb dissolving in the innermost recesses of my soul.

—*Blessed Henry Suso, O.P.* (+1365)

15. Give me, O glorious Virgin, the strength, talent, and speech,
that I may announce to the faithful and to your clients the glory
of your name. Not how much it is, nor what it is; but that I, your
little servant, may tell something of your immense praises, to
your glory, to my devotion and the solace of all the readers.

—*St. Bernardine of Siena, O.F.M.* (+1444)

16. The devils fear the Queen of Heaven to such a degree, that
only on hearing her great name pronounced, they fly from him
who does so as from a burning fire.

—*Venerable Thomas a Kempis* (+1471)

17. After the most holy and adorable Name of Jesus, there is no name more glorious or more powerful than the name of Mary. At the mention of this name, the angels rejoice and the devils tremble; through this invocation of this name, sinners obtain grace and pardon.

—*St. Peter Canisius, S.J.*
Doctor of the Church (+1597)

18. As often as the sweet name of Mary comes to your lips, you ought to represent to yourself a masterpiece of God's power, so perfect and so sublime that even the arm of the Almighty could not produce anything more perfect in the shape of a pure creature.

—*St. Leonard of Port Maurice, O.F.M.* (+1751)

19. Salvation is occasionally more easily obtained, says St. Anselm (*De Excell. Virg.*, c. 6) by calling on the Name of Mary than by invoking that of Jesus. Not that He is not the source and Lord of all graces, but because, when we have recourse to the Mother, and she prays for us, her prayers have greater efficacy than ours, as being those of a mother.

—*St. Alphonsus Liguori, C.SS.R., Bp. C.*
Doctor of the Church (+1787)

IV

Presentation of the Holy Child Mary

1. *Hearken, O daughter, and see, and incline your ear; and forget your people and your father's house; and the King shall greatly desire your beauty* (Ps. 44:11-12). *Arise, make haste, My love, My dove, My beautiful one, and come.* (Cant. 2:10).

2. O God Who was pleased that on this day the Blessed Mary ever Virgin, the dwelling-place of the Holy Ghost, should be

presented in the Temple: grant, we beseech you, that through her prayers we may be found worthy to be presented in the temple of your glory. Through Our Lord...in the unity of the same...

—A *Collect for the Mass of the Presentation*, 21 November

3. Anne did not long delay leading her to the temple, and offering her to God.

—*St. Gregory of Nyssa* (+403)

4. Hers was the hidden treasure of modesty, hers the self sacrifice of earnestness, hers to be the pattern of maidenhood at home, of kinswomanhood in ministry, of motherhood in the temple. O how many virgins has she presented to the Lord, saying: "Here is one who (like me) has kept stainlessly clean the wedding chamber."

—*St. Ambrose, Bp. C. Doctor of the Church* (+397)

5. In her third year she was brought to the temple.

—*St. Epiphanius, Ab. Bp. C.* (+403)

6. Go, then, O Queen of the world, O Mother of God, go joyfully to the house of God, there to await the coming of the Divine Spirit, Who will make you the Mother of the Eternal Word. Enter with exultation the courts of the Lord.

—*St. Germanus of Constantinople, Bp. C.* (+c. 732)

V

Adornments of Her Soul

1. *She is more precious than all riches: and all the things that are desired are not to be compared with her. Her ways are beautiful ways, and all her paths are peaceable. She is a tree of life to them that lay hold of her: and he that shall retain her is blessed.*

—(Prov. 3:15, 17, 18)

2. The evil done by Eve's incredulity was remedied by Mary's faith.

—*St. Irenaeus, Bp. M.* (+c. 202)

3. You, O Mary, have been made the holy one, and more glorious, more pure, and more saintly than all the rest of humankind, having a mind whiter than snow, and your soul more purified than the finest gold.

—*St. Gregory Thaumaturgus, Bp. C.* (+c. 270)

4. Let the life of the blessed Mary be ever present to you, in which, as in a mirror, the beauty of chastity and form of virtue shine forth. She was a virgin not only in body, but in mind, who never sullied the pure affection of her heart by unworthy feelings. She was humble of heart, serious in her conversation, prudent in her counsels, fonder of reading than of speaking. She placed her confidence rather in the prayer of the poor, than in the uncertain riches of this world. She was ever intent in her occupations, reserved in her conversation, and accustomed to make God, rather than man, the witness of her thoughts...her very appearance was the picture of her mind and the figure of piety.

—*St. Ambrose, Bp. C.*
Doctor of the Church (+397)

5.   She was a virgin, not in body only, but in mind also; the purity of her thoughts had been deflowered by no evil suggestion, she was lowly in heart.... So pure was Blessed Mary that she was (chosen) to be the Mother of the Lord; God made her whom He had chosen, and chose her of whom He would be made.

—*St. Ambrose, Bp. C.*
Doctor of the Church (+397)

6.   If you look diligently at Mary, there is nothing of virtue, nothing of beauty, nothing of splendor or glory which does not shine in her.

—*St. Jerome, Pr. C.*
Doctor of the Church (+420)

7.   Of the Blessed Virgin Mary, for the honor of Christ, when we treat of sin I do not wish that she should be involved. For we know that a greater grace was accorded her wholly to conquer sin, by the very fact that she merited to conceive and bear Him of Whom we certainly know that He had no sin.

—*St.Augustine, Bp. C.*
Doctor of the Church (+430)

8.   God chose this most pure virgin for His Mother, that she might be an example of chastity to all.

—*St. Sophronius* (+c. 640)

9.   He Who said, *Honor your father and your mother*, that He might observe His own decree gave all grace and honor to His Mother.

—*St. Methodius, C.* (+847)

10. As the light of the sun so greatly surpasses that of the stars, that in it they are no longer visible, it so overwhelms them that

they are as if they were not; so does the great Virgin Mother surpass in sanctity the whole court of Heaven.

—*St. Peter Damian, Bp. C.*
Doctor of the Church (+1072)

11. It was only fitting that the Virgin to whose care God the Father was pleased to confide His only Son, should shine with a dazzling purity, surpassing all but that of God Himself.

—*St. Anselm, O.S.B., Bp. C.*
Doctor of the Church (+1109)

12. *Ave, gratia plena.* It was not enough for the Archangel simply to commend the grace of Mary; he wished also to insist emphatically on its fullness, when he said *Gratia plena*. O truly full, and fully full! Gabriel had not yet said: *Behold, you shall conceive in the womb.* He had not yet said: *The Holy Ghost shall come upon you.* If, therefore, *before* the coming upon her of the Holy Ghost, *before* the conception of the Son of God, Mary was full of grace, how much more so afterwards? Therefore St. Anselm aptly says of her fullness and of the fullness of her gratitude, "She, being already a thousand times full (of grace), was saluted by the Angel, filled with the Holy Ghost, breathed upon by the Divine plenitude." Well, therefore, is Mary said to be full of the (nine plenitudes, viz.) illumination of wisdom, of the outpouring of grace, of the riches of a good life, of the unction of mercy, of the perfection of the Church, of the redolence of fair fame, of the resplendence of divine glory, of the joy of eternal gladness.

—*St. Bonaventure, O.F.M., Bp. C.*
Doctor of the Church (+1274)

13. Fitly is she compared to the aurora as well for herself as for us; for herself especially, for us in general. Mary for herself is well compared to the aurora according to Scripture: first, because of the driving away of the night of sin; secondly, because of the approach of the light of grace; third, because of the

rising of the Sun of Justice; fourth, because of the place of her throne of glory. First in her most full sanctification; secondly in her most bright conversation; thirdly, in her most wonderful generation of her Son; fourthly, in her most glorious Assumption.

—*St. Bonaventure, O.F.M., Bp. C.*
Doctor of the Church (+1274)

14. Because Mary was free from original sin, she found no obstacle in obeying God; she was like a wheel, which was easily turned by every inspiration of the Holy Ghost.

—*St. Bonaventure, O.F.M., Bp. C.*
Doctor of the Church (+1274)

15. *Grace is shed abroad on your lips.* Such was the grace of the lips of Mary, that she could excellently be prefigured by Judith, of whom it is said, *There is not another woman upon earth in look, in beauty, and in sense of words* (Judith 11:19). Truly there is not, nor ever was, nor ever will be, such another woman upon earth, as Mary was, in her glorious life, in the beauty of a pure conscience, and in the sense of words of a most skilled tongue. We shall clearly see the grace of the lips in Mary if we diligently gather and meditate the words of her lips as recorded in the Gospel.

—*St. Bonaventure, O.F.M., Bp. C.*
Doctor of the Church (+1274)

16. Her sanctification (from before her birth) was more perfect than that of others. We must hold that all that could be accorded to her was in fact accorded. It is altogether probable that she who bore the only Son of the Father, full of grace and truth, in preference to all others received greater privileges and graces.

—*St. Thomas Aquinas, O.P., C.*
Doctor of the Church (+1274)

17. *He has set My tabernacle in the sun* (Ps. 18:6). This means that Christ caused His body to rest in the sun, that is in the Blessed Virgin who had no darkening of sin, according to the word of the Canticle: *You are all beautiful, My beloved, there is no spot in you.*

—*St. Thomas Aquinas, O.P., C.*
Doctor of the Church (+1274)

18. Inasmuch as the Blessed Virgin is the Mother of God, she possesses infinite dignity, derived from the infinite perfections of God, and in this respect, nothing superior to her can be made, since the omnipotence of God cannot bestow a greater honor on a mere creature.

—*St. Thomas Aquinas, O.P., C.*
Doctor of the Church (+1274)

19. Let the teacher in our order always imitate the example of Mary. Thus he shall be able to make his students into so many true brethren of Jesus.

—*St. Joseph Calasanctius* (+1648)

20. With reason is Mary called the Virgin of virgins: for she, without the counsel or example of others, was the first who offered her virginity to God.

—*St. Albertus Magnus, O.P., Pr. C.*
Doctor of the Church (+1280)

21. As flies are driven away by a great fire, so were the evil spirits driven away by her ardent love (for God); so much so, that they did not even dare approach her.

—*St. Bernardine of Siena, O.F.M.* (+1444)

22. Nothing was ever granted to any saint which did not shine in

a much higher degree in Mary from the very first moment of her existence.

—*St. Thomas of Villanova, O.S.A.* (+1555)

23. This faithful handmaid never, in thought or word or deed, contradicted the Most High, but, entirely despoiled of her own will, she lived always and in all things obedient to that of God.

—*St. Thomas of Villanova, O.S.A.* (+1555)

25. As the charity of this Mother of love excels in perfection that of all the Saints in Heaven, so did she exercise it more perfectly.... She never felt any contradiction from the sensual appetite, and therefore her love, as a true Solomon, reigned peaceably in her soul and made all its acts at its pleasure.

—*St. Francis de Sales, Bp. C.*
Doctor of the Church (+1622)

24. Her charity surpassed that of the Seraphim, for *many daughters have gathered together riches: you have surpassed them all* (Prov. 31:29). The Saints and Angels are but compared to stars, and the first of them to the fairest of the stars; but she is fair as the moon, as easy to be chosen and discerned from all the Saints as the sun from the stars. And going on further I think again that as the charity of this Mother of love excels in perfection that of all the Saints in Heaven, so did she exercise it more perfectly, I say even in this mortal life. She never sinned venially, as the Church agrees; she had then no change nor delay in the way of love, but by a perpetual advancement ascended from love to love.

—*St. Francis de Sales, Bp. C.*
Doctor of the Church (+1622)

26. It is certain that Mary's soul was the most beautiful that God had ever created; nay, more, after the work of the Incarnation of the Eternal Word, this was the greatest and most

worthy of Himself that an omnipotent God ever did in the world.

—St. Alphonsus Liguori, C.SS.R., Bp. C.
Doctor of the Church (+1787)

27. *Who is she that goes forth by the desert, as a pillar of smoke, of aromatical spices, of myrrh, and frankincense, and all the powders of the perfumer?* (Cant. 8:6). Her entire mortification typified by the myrrh, her fervent prayers signified by the incense, and all her holy virtues united to her perfect love for God, kindled in her a flame so great that her beautiful soul, wholly devoted to and consumed by divine love, arose continually to God as a pillar of smoke, breathing forth on every side a most sweet odor. Eustachius (Patriarch of Constantinople, 10th century) wrote, "A pillar of smoke, because burning interiorly as a holocaust with the flame of divine love, she sent forth a most sweet odor."

—St. Alphonsus Liguori, C.SS.R., Bp. C.
Doctor of the Church (+1787)

28. O Holy Mary, paradise of sanctity, lily of purity, be my guide and the defender of my chastity: for in you shines every grace of life and truth.

—St. Gertrude the Great, O.S.B., V. (+1301)

29. We beseech you, Lord, that the Blessed Virgin, blooming rose without a thorn, gleaming lily without a stain, flowery garden for all kinds of virtues, through whom our poverty is alleviated and enriched, be ever our perpetual advocate near you.

—St. Gertrude the Great, O.S.B., V. (+1301)

30. Hail Lady, saintly and sacred Queen, Mary, Mother of God, perpetual Virgin, chosen by the eternal Father, his beloved Son

and the Holy Spirit, Consoler.

In you is and was all plenitude of grace and every good.

Hail, God's palace; Hail, Tabernacle of the Most High; Hail, House of God; Hail, his Holy vestments; Hail, handmaid of God.

Hail, Mother of God.

—*St. Francis of Assisi, C. (+1226)*

31. O Most Holy Virgin Mary, there never was born among women anyone like you, Daughter and Handmaid of the Most High King and Heavenly Father; Heavenly Mother of Our Lord Jesus Christ; Spouse of the Holy Spirit. Together with St. Michael and with all the powers of heaven and with all the saints, pray for us to your Most Holy Son, Our Lord and Master. Amen.

—*St. Francis of Assisi, C. (+1226)*

VI

Attributes and Qualities of Mary

1. Mary is the glory of virgins, the joy of mothers, the support of the faithful, the diadem of the Church, the express model of the true Faith, the seat of piety, the robe of virtue, the dwelling-place of the Holy Trinity.

—*St. Proclus, Patriarch of Constantinople (+446)*

2. Consider how Mary is full of the joy of eternal happiness. Who is ignorant that she is of those of whom her Son said: *Ask, and you shall receive, that your joy may be full?* If, therefore, the joy of the Apostles, of all those who are reigning with God, is full,

how much more is the joy of the Mother of God full and complete? Of this plenitude St. Jerome says: "Full indeed of grace, full of God, full of virtues, she could not but possess most fully the glory of eternal splendor." What wonder, then, that she has full and overfull joy and glory in the Kingdom, who had grace full and overflowing in her exile upon earth? What wonder if both in Heaven and on earth her fullness was above that of every creature from whose fullness every creature has life?

—St. Bonaventure, O.F.M., Bp. C.
Doctor of the Church (+1274)

3.   Sanctifying grace not only repressed all irregular motions in the Blessed Virgin herself, but was also efficacious for others; so that notwithstanding the greatness of her beauty, she was never coveted by others.

—St. Thomas Aquinas, O.P., C.
Doctor of the Church (+1274)

4.   In this Shewing He brought Our Blessed Lady to my understanding. I saw her ghostly, in bodily likeness: a simple maid and meek, young of age, and little waxen above a child, in the stature that she was when she conceived. Also God shewed in part the wisdom and the truth of her soul: wherein I understood the reverent beholding in which she beheld her God and Maker, marvelling with great reverence that He would be born of her that was a simple creature of His making. And this wisdom and truth—knowing the greatness of her Maker and the littleness of herself that was made—caused her to say full meekly to Gabriel: Lo me, God's handmaid! In this sight I understood truly that she is more than all that God made beneath her in worthiness and grace; for above her is nothing that is made but the blessed Manhood of Christ, as to my sight.

—Blessed Dame Julian of Norwich (+c. 1415)

5.   For this reason she was called myrrh, which prevents corruption, in the words of Ecclesiasticus, applied to her by the
Church: *I yielded a sweet odor like the best myrrh* (Ecclus. 24:20;
and see *Off. B.V.M.*, resp. 4).

—*St. Alphonsus Liguori, C.SS.R., Bp. C.*
Doctor of the Church (+1787)

6.   The Virgin Mary is given to us as an example of obedience
as she says: Behold the handmaid of the Lord, be it done unto
me according to your word.

—*St. Irenaeus, Bp. M.* (+c. 202)

7.   The knot tied by Eve's disobedience, was untied by the
obedience of Mary.

—*St. Irenaeus, Bp. M.* (+c. 202)

8.   God said to her: "In my goodness, I set up Mary as a sort of
bite, to catch the rational souls of men."

—*St. Catherine of Siena, V.*
Doctor of the Church (+1380)

9.   O blessed and most holy Virgin, who were the first among
all women to consecrate your virginity to God by a perpetual
vow, and were because of this granted to become the Mother of
his Only-Begotten Son, I entreat your unspeakable goodness to
disregard my sins and defects, and to grant me that I may have
for Spouse the beloved of my soul, the Most Holy Son of God
and your child, my Lord Jesus Christ!

—*St. Catherine of Siena, V.*
Doctor of the Church (+1380)

10. You, O Mary, are the young plant that produced the fragrant flower of the Word, Only-Begotten of God, because you were the fertile land that was sown with this Word.

—*St. Catherine of Siena, V.*
Doctor of the Church (+1380)

11. I have recourse to you, dear Mary, and I place before you my petition in behalf of the Church, the sweet Spouse of Christ, your ineffable Son, and in behalf of his Vicar on earth, the Holy Father, so that light may be given to him to wisely and prudently reform the Holy Church.

—*St. Catherine of Siena, V.*
Doctor of the Church (+1380)

12. *The Lord is with you,* with you in mind, with you in the womb, with you in the nuptial chamber, with you in the exalted castle. Outstanding indeed is the grace of Mary, superabundant and flowing over, so as to give glory to the heavens, beget God on the earth, fill the Angels with joy, and bring peace to the world.

—*St. Laurence Justinian* (+1455)

13. While Eve was seduced by the words of an evil angel to flee from God betraying his word; Mary was evangelized by the words of a good angel so as to ascend to God obeying his word. The former appears disobedient to God, the latter, on the contrary, docile to Divine Wisdom, obeyed so perfectly that the Virgin Mary became the advocate of the virgin Eve. Thus, as mankind was handed over unto death by a virgin, so also by a Virgin it has been saved. The obedience of a Virgin compensates for the disobedience of another.

—*St. Irenaeus, Bp. M.* (+c. 202)

14. She is of all creatures the one closest to God by reason of the flesh. She is also the one closest to him by way of charity. And

just as iron, when placed in the fire, becomes completely taken
over by it, so that it almost looks like fire, so also this Blessed
Virgin, placed in the furnace of divine love, became so full of it
and so much like it, that she could truly become the Mother of
the whole Christian people, so much so that, in comparison
with her, all other mothers do not deserve the name of mother.

—*St. John of Avila* (+1569)

15. We find ourselves in this earth as in a tempestuous sea, in a
desert, in a vale of tears. Now then, Mary is the Star of the Sea,
the solace of our desert, the light that guides us towards Heaven.

—*St. John Bosco* (+1888)

VII

Other Tributes and Observations

1.   How rightly, too, has every nation and every liturgy without exception acclaimed her great renown, which has grown
greater with the voice of each succeeding century. Among her
many other titles we find her hailed as Our Lady, Our Mediatrix
(St. Bernard: *Serm. II in advent. Domini*, n. 5), the repairer of the
whole world in ruins (St. Tharasius: *Orat. in praesentat. Dei-
parae*), the dispenser (Conciliatrix) of God's gifts (Office of the
Greek Church, 8 December, Theotokion after hymn IX).

—*Pope Leo XIII* (+1903)

2.   Hail, reconciler of the whole world!

—*St. Ephraem of Edessa*
Doctor of the Church (+c. 373)

3.   Evil came by a woman, so good has come by the Woman:
for by Eve we fell, by Mary we stand; by Eve we were reduced to

slavery, by Mary we were made free. Eve took from us length of days, Mary restored to us immortality; Eve caused us to be condemned by the fruit of the tree, Mary wrought our pardon by the gift of the Tree, because Christ also hung upon the Tree as Fruit. As therefore we died through a tree, so by a Tree are we brought to life. All that was done by Adam is washed out by Mary.

—St. Ambrose, Bp. C.
Doctor of the Church (+397)

4.   Queen of the world...the tabernacle of God...the celestial ladder by which the King of Heaven descended to earth, and man ascends to Heaven.

—St. Peter Damian, Bp. C.
Doctor of the Church (+1072)

5.   It was only fitting that the Virgin to whose care God the Father was pleased to confide His only Son, should shine with a dazzling purity, surpassing all but that of God.

—St. Anselm, O.S.B., Bp. C.
Doctor of the Church (+1109)

6.   Jesus and Mary, my most sweet loves, for you may I suffer, for you may I die; grant that I may be in all things yours and in nothing mine.

—St. Alphonsus Rodriquez, S.J. (+1617)

7.   How can I help loving her, if she is my mother!

—St. Stanislaus Kostka, S.J. (+1568)

8.   O my Lady, Holy Mary, hope of all Christians, Queen of Angels and of all of God's Saints in Heaven.

—St. Francis Xavier, S.J., C. (+1552)

9. I remember that when my mother died I was twelve years old or a little less. When I began to understand what I had lost, I went, afflicted, before an image of Our Lady and besought her with many tears to be my mother. It seems to me that although I did this in simplicity it helped me. For I have found favor with this sovereign Virgin in everything I have asked of her and in the end she has drawn me to herself.

—*St. Teresa of Avila*
Doctor of the Church (+1582)

10. The beauty that I saw in Our Lady was extraordinary, although I didn't make out any particular details except the form of her face in general and that her garment was of the most brilliant white, not dazzling but soft. Our Lady seemed to me to be a very young girl.

—*St. Teresa of Avila*
Doctor of the Chruch (+1582)

11. We begin our apostolic service by invoking as a resplendent star on our way, the Mother of God, Mary, *Salus Populi* and *Mater Ecclesiae*, whom the liturgy venerates in a special way this month of September. May Our Lady who guided with delicate tenderness our life as a boy, as a seminarian, as a priest and as a bishop continue to enlighten and direct our steps in order that as Peter's voice and with our eyes and mind fixed on her Son, Jesus, we may proclaim in the world with joyous firmness our profession of faith: You are Christ, the Son of the living God (Mt. 16:16).

—*Pope John Paul I* (+1978)

12. What shall I do when tempted by the flesh? Have the Virgin for your advocate, who is a fragrance of sweet smelling incense, wafting through the squares. . . . She has the fragrance of myrrh that destroys the worms of corruption. If you are devoted to her, you will feel temptations melting away, like wax before the fire.

—*St. John of Avila* (+1569)

13. It is one of the signs of those who are to be saved to have a great devotion to Mary.

—*St. John of Avila* (+1569)

14. O Mary, the sweet wounds of Jesus and your atrocious sorrows are forever impressed on my heart!

—*St. Gabriel of the Most Sorrowful Virgin* (+1862)

15. If we have Mary, we possess everything. If we don't, we lack everything. If Mary defends us, who will be able to do us any harm?

—*St. Gabriel of the Most Sorrowful Virgin* (+1862)

16. Who did ever come away from her company sick or downcast, or devoid of some knowledge of the heavenly mysteries?

—*St. Amadeus, Cist.* (+1159)

17. Who did ever return home bereft of joy, after having entreated Mary, Mother of God, in behalf of his needs?

—*St. Amadeus, Cist.* (+1159)

VIII

Espousals of Our Lady

1.   The special motives for which St. Joseph has been proclaimed Patron of the Church . . . are that Joseph was the spouse of Mary and that he was reputed the father of Jesus Christ. From these sources have sprung his dignity, his holiness, his glory. The dignity of the Mother of God is so lofty that naught created can rank above it. But as Joseph has been united to the Blessed Virgin by the ties of marriage, it may not be doubted that he approached nearer than anyone else to the eminent dignity by which the Mother of God so nobly surpasses all

created natures. For marriage is the most intimate of all unions, which from its essence imparts a community of gifts between those joined together by it. Thus, in giving Joseph the Blessed Virgin as spouse, God appointed him to be, not only her life's companion, but also, by virtue of the conjugal tie, a participator in her sublime dignity.

—*Pope Leo XIII* (+1903)

2.   You say Mary did not remain a virgin: I go much further and say that Joseph too was a virgin for Mary's sake, that of a virginal marriage a Virgin Son might be born.

—*St. Jerome, Pr. C.*
Doctor of the Church (+420)

3.   *Our Lady's Espousals*

Wife did she live, yet virgin die,
Untouched by man, yet mother of a son;
To save herself and child from fatal lie,
To end the web whereof the thread was spun,
In marriage knot to Joseph she was tied,
Unwonted works with wonted veils to hide.

God lent His paradise to Joseph's care,
Wherein He was to plant the tree of life;
His son, of Joseph's child the title bear,
Just cause to make the mother Joseph's wife.
Oh blessed man! betrothed to such a spouse,
More blessed to live with such a child in house!

No carnal love this sacred league procured,
All vain delights were far from their assent;
Thou both in wedlock bands themselves assured,
Yet straight by vow they sealed their chaste intent.
Thus had she virgin's, wife's and widow's crown,
And by chaste childbirth doubled her renown.

—*St. Robert Southwell, S.J., M.* (+1595)

IX

Annunciation—Incarnation

1. *Then the Creator of all things commanded, and said to me: and He that made me rested in my tabernacle.*

—*(Ecclus.* 24:12)

2. The Eternal Son of God, about to take upon Him our nature for the saving and ennobling of man, and about to consummate thus a mystical union between Himself and all mankind, did not accomplish His design without adding thereto the free consent of the elect Mother, who represented in some sort all humankind, according to the illustrious and just opinion of St. Thomas (Aquinas, O.P., Doctor of the Church, +1274), who says that the Annunciation was effected with the consent of the Virgin standing in the place of humanity (S. Th. III, q. 30, a. I).

—*Pope Leo XIII* (+1903)

3. Hail full of grace, you are the golden urn containing the Manna from Heaven!

—*St. Epiphanius, Ab. Bp. C.* (+403)

4. Answer, O Sacred Virgin, why delay you the salvation of the world, which depends on your consent?

—*St. Augustine, Bp. C.*
Doctor of the Church (+430)

5. The Virgin's festival incites our tongue today to herald her praise. Mary is the handmaid and Mother, Virgin and Heaven, the only bridge of God to men, the awful loom of the Incarnation, in which by some unspeakable way the garment of that union was woven, whereof the weaver is the Holy Ghost; and the spinner the overshadowing from on high; the wool the

ancient fleece of Adam; the woof the undefiled flesh from the Virgin; the weaver's shuttle the immense grace of Him Who brought it about; the artificer the Word gliding through the hearing.

—*St. Proclus, Patriarch of Constantinople* (+446)

6.   *Fear not, Mary, you have found grace with God.* As Christ was pleased to be comforted by an angel, so was it necessary that the Virgin should be encouraged by one.

—*St. Peter Chrysologus, Bp. C.*
Doctor of the Church (+c. 450)

7.   *He has hidden me in His tabernacle* (Ps. 26:5). The tabernacle is Mary, a tabernacle made by God, in which He alone entered to accomplish the great work of the Redemption of man.

—*St. Germanus of Constantinople, Bp. C.* (+c. 732)

8.   *Hail, full of grace!* (Luke 1:28). In her womb was the grace of divinity, in her heart the grace of charity, upon her lips the grace of courtesy, in her hands the grace of mercy and gener-osity. And she was truly full of grace, for of her captives have received redemption, the sick their cure, the sorrowful their comfort, and sinners their pardon; the just have received grace, the angels joy, and the Blessed Trinity glory and honor, and the Son of Man the substance of human flesh. *The Lord is with you* (loc. cit.). God the Father is with you, Whom you clothe and surround with your flesh. O Virgin, make haste to give your answer! Answer a word and receive the Word, utter your own word and receive the Word of God, pronounce a word that shall pass and embrace a Word that shall not pass, arise, run, be opened! Arise by faith, run by devotion, be opened by your consent.

—*St. Bernard of Clairvaux, Cist.*
Doctor of the Church (+1153)

9. *Behold, you shall conceive in your womb, and shall bring forth a Son: and you shall call His Name Jesus* (Luke 1:31). The angel awaits the reply and we also, O Lady, on whom the sentence of condemnation weighs so heavily, await the word of mercy. Behold, the price of our salvation is offered you; we shall be instantly delivered if you consent. For the Lord Himself desires your consent, by which He has determined to save the world.

—*St. Bernard of Clairvaux, Cist.*
Doctor of the Church (+1153)

10. The Archangel Gabriel by saluting the glorious Virgin Mary with a glorious salutation, most fittingly consummated her blessedness by saying, *Blessed are you among women*, that is, more blessed than all women. And by this, whatever of malediction was infused into our nature by Eve, was taken away by the blessing of Mary. Let Gabriel therefore say, "Blessed are you among women"; blessed, I say, because of the fullness of grace to be venerated in you; blessed, because of the greatness of the mercy to be bestowed by you; blessed, because of the Majesty of the Person Who is to take flesh of you; blessed, because of the weight of glory which is to be accumulated in you.

—*St. Bonaventure, O.F.M., Bp. C.*
Doctor of the Church (+1274)

11. The chief and immediate disposition of Mary at her conceiving (of Jesus) was the sincerity of love in her heart, which disposed her to receive the love of the Holy Ghost, in order that she might conceive the immaculate Son.

—*St. Bonaventure, O.F.M., Bp. C.*
Doctor of the Church (+1274)

12. *Fear not, Mary, for you have found grace with God* (Luke 1:30). Fear not, O Mary, for you have found, not taken grace, as Lucifer tried to take it; you have not lost it, as Adam lost it; you

have not bought it, as Simon Magus would have bought it; but
you have found it because you have desired and sought it. You
have found uncreated grace: that is, God Himself became your
Son; and with that grace you have found and obtained every
created good.

> —*St. Albertus Magnus, O.P., Pr. C.*
> *Doctor of the Church* (+1280)

13. Had the angel said, O Mary, you are the greatest sinner in
the world, her astonishment would not have been so great; the
sound of so high praises filled her with fear.

> —*St. Bernardine of Siena, O.F.M.* (+1444)

14. When the Triune God destined and elevated a mortal
Virgin to the dignity of Mother of the Redeemer, the Father
must of necessity have endowed her with a plenitude of perfection suitable for such a dignity. The Son, the Eternal Wisdom
of God, in choosing her for His Mother, bestowed on her as
much wisdom as was necessary to establish between Mother
and Son a comparative equality; that is, He imparted to her a
certain immensity of grace and perfection, so that as the Virgin
gave Christ His human nature, Christ, in a certain sense, divi-
nized Mary. And the Holy Ghost Who descended upon her in
the Incarnation with all His fullness, must have conferred upon
her such treasures of sanctity as would fit her to receive the
Holy of Holies in her most pure womb. In reality, Mary possessed, according to the declaration of the Archangel, such a
fullness of grace, that she was worthy to become the Mother of
God.

> —*St. Bernardine of Siena, O.F.M.* (+1444)

15. O powerful *Fiat!* O *Fiat* to be venerated above every other
fiat! For with a *fiat* God created light, heaven, earth; but with
Mary's *fiat*, God became Man.

> —*St. Thomas of Villanova, O.S.A.* (+1555)

16. *Behold the handmaid of the Lord; be it done unto me according to your word* (Luke 1:38). What more beautiful, more humble, or more prudent answer could all the wisdom of men and angels together have invented, had they reflected for a million years? O powerful answer, which rejoiced Heaven and brought an immense sea of graces and blessings into the world!—answer which had scarcely fallen from the lips of Mary, before it drew the only-begotten Son of God from the bosom of His Eternal Father, to become Man in her most pure womb! Yes, indeed; for scarcely had she uttered these words when instantly *the Word was made flesh* (John 1:14): the Son of God became also the Son of Mary.

—*St. Alphonsus Liguori, C.SS.R., Bp. C. Doctor of the Church* (+1787)

17. St. Thomas Aquinas calls the mystery of the Incarnation of the Eternal Word "the miracle of miracles" (*De Pot.*, 1. 6, a. 2). What greater prodigy could the world behold, than a woman become the Mother of God, and a God clothed in human flesh? Mary, by her humility, became the Mother of her Creator. The Creator, in His goodness, became the Son of His own creature.

—*St. Alphonsus Liguori, C.SS.R., Bp. C. Doctor of the Church* (+1787)

18. *Hail, full of grace; the Lord is with you; blessed are you among women* (Luke 1:28). Hail, O Virgin full of grace; for you were always full of grace above all other saints. The Lord is with you because you are so humble. You are blessed among women, for all others fall under the curse of sin; but you, because you are the Mother of the Blessed One, are, and always you will be blessed and free from stain.

—*St. Alphonsus Liguori, C.SS.R., Bp. C. Doctor of the Church* (+1787)

19. O God, Who was pleased that Your Word should take flesh

at the message of an angel in the womb of the Blessed Virgin
Mary, grant to us your suppliants, that we who believe her to be
truly the Mother of God may be helped by her intercession with
You. Through the same...

—*A Collect for a Mass for Lady Day*

20. So soon as the Blessed Virgin Mary expressed her assent to
the angel's words by saying *Behold the handmaid of the Lord, be it
done unto me according to your word*, then immediately, that is in
the very first instant, the most holy Body of Christ was, by the
power of the Holy Spirit, formed of the most pure womb of the
Blessed Virgin Mary, a human soul created out of nothing was
joined to that body, and the Godhead joined to the body and
the soul. Whence it came to pass that in the same instant of time
there existed perfect God and perfect Man, so that the Blessed
Virgin Mary could be truly and rightly called Mother of God
and of man, for in that same instant she conceived a man who
was God.

—*Catechism of the Council of Trent (1545-1563)*

21. The Hail Mary is the most beautiful of all prayers after the
Our Father. It is the most perfect compliment which you can
make to Mary, because it is the compliment which the Most
High sent her by an archangel, in order to win her Heart; and it
was so powerful over her Heart by the secret charms of which it
is so full, that in spite of her profound humility she gave her
consent to the Incarnation of the Word. It is by this compliment also that you will infallibly win her Heart, if you say it as
you ought. The Hail Mary well said—that is, with attentive
devotion and modesty (and, he could have added, said *slowly*
and most reverently, with the mind on each sublime word)—is,
according to the saints, the enemy of the devil which puts him
to flight, and the hammer which crushes him. It is the sanctification of the soul, the joy of the angels, the melody of the pre-
destinate, the canticle of the New Testament, the pleasure of
Mary, and the glory of the most Holy Trinity. The Hail Mary is

a heavenly dew which fertilizes the soul. It is the chaste and loving kiss which we give to Mary. It is a vermillion rose which we present to her; a precious pearl we offer her; a chalice of divine ambrosial nectar which we hold to her. All these are comparisons of the saints.

—*St. Louis-Marie Grignon de Montfort* (+1716)

22. When Mary Immaculate, the finest and most fragrant flower of all creation said in answer to the angel's greeting: "Behold the handmaid of the Lord," she accepted the honor of divine motherhood, which was in that moment realized within her. And we, born once in our father Adam, formerly the adopted sons of God but fallen from that high estate, are now once more brothers, adopted sons of the Father, restored to his adoption by the redemption which has already begun. At the foot of the Cross, we shall be the children of Mary, with that same Jesus whom she conceived at the Annunciation. From today onwards, she will be the Mother of God and our Mother too.

—*Pope John XXIII* (+1963)

X

Holy Humility of Mary

1.   God chose her to be His Mother more on account of her humility than of all her other sublime virtues.

—*St. Jerome, Pr. C.*
Doctor of the Church (+420)

2.   Mary's humility became a heavenly ladder, by which God came into the world.

—*St. Augustine, Bp. C.*
Doctor of the Church (+430)

3.   Mary never exalted herself by reason of heavenly gifts; as she became more and more acquainted with heavenly mysteries, she fixed her mind more firmly in humility, answering the Angel, *Behold the handmaid of the Lord* (Luke 1:38). This is an example to many, who in honors and prosperity, in graces and virtues, do not humble themselves with Mary and with Christ, but grow elated with pride like Eve and Lucifer.

—*St. Bede the Venerable, O.S.B.*
Doctor of the Church (+735)

4.   Though she pleased by her virginity, she conceived by her humility.

—*St. Bernard of Clairvaux, Cist.*
Doctor of the Church (+1153)

5.   And how, Our Lady, could you unite in your heart so humble an opinion of yourself with so great purity, with such innocence, and so great a plenitude of grace as you did possess? And how, O blessed one, did this humility and so great humility ever take so deep root in your heart, seeing yourself thus honored and exalted by God?

—*St. Bernard of Clairvaux, Cist.*
Doctor of the Church (+1153)

6.   You would never have ascended far above all the choirs of angels, if on earth you had not lowered yourself by humility below all men.

—*St. Bernard of Clairvaux, Cist.*
Doctor of the Church (+1153)

7.   O humility! as nothing in its own eyes, yet sufficiently great for the Divinity! Insufficient for itself, sufficient for Him Whom the heavens cannot contain.

—*Blessed Guerric, Cist.*
Ab. of Igny (+1157)

8. In all temptations of pride, there is no greater remedy than this one: to have recourse to the humble Jesus and Mary.

—*St. Alphonsus Rodriquez, S.J.* (+1617)

9. *And there shall come forth a rod out of the root of Jesse, and a flower shall rise up out of his root,* (Isaias 11:1). The only-begotten Son of God was to be born, not from the summit, nor from the trunk of the tree, but from the root, precisely to denote the humility of the Mother: by the root humility of heart is understood.

—*St. Albertus Magnus, O.P., Pr. C.*
Doctor of the Church (+1280)

10. Remark that the flower rises, not from the summit, but out of the root.

—*Blessed Raymond Jordano, Ab.* (+1381)

11. *He has regarded the humility of His handmaid* (Magnificat). She did not say, He has regarded the virginity or the innocence, but only the humility, of His handmaid.

—*St. Laurence Justinian* (+1455)

12. *While the King was at His repose, my spikenard sent forth the odor thereof* (Cant. 1:2). Spikenard, from its being a small and lowly herb, was a type of Mary, who in the highest degree gave forth the sweet odor of her humility.

—*St. Antoninus, O.P., Bp. C.* (+1459)

13. The last grace of perfection is preparation for the conception of the Son of God, which preparation is made by profound humility.

—*St. Antoninus, O.P., Bp. C.* (+1459)

XI

Spouse of God the Holy Spirit

1.   Among the external operations of God, the highest of all is
the mystery of the Incarnation. . . . Now this work, though it
belongs to the whole Trinity, is appropriated especially to the
Holy Ghost, so that the Gospels thus speak of the Blessed
Virgin: *She was found with child, of the Holy Ghost,* and *That
which is conceived in her, is of the Holy Ghost* (Mt. 1:18-20). And
this is rightly ascribed to Him, Who is the love of the Father and
the Son, since this great "mystery of godliness" (1 Tm. 3:16)
proceeds from the infinite love of God towards man, as St. John
(3:16) tells us: *God so loved the world, as to give His only-begotten
Son.*

—*Pope Leo XIII* (+1903)

2.   Mary was the only one who merited to be called the Mother
and Spouse of God.

—*St. Augustine, Bp. C.*
Doctor of the Church (+430)

3.   The Divine Spirit, the love itself of the Father and the Son,
came corporally into Mary, and enriching her with graces above
all creatures, reposed in her and made her His Spouse, the
Queen of Heaven and earth.

—*St. Anselm, O.S.B., Bp. C.*
Doctor of the Church (+1109)

4.   *The Holy Ghost shall come upon you* (Luke 1:35). Mary is
called the temple of the Lord and the sacred resting-place of the
Holy Ghost: for by the operation of the Holy Ghost she became
the Mother of the Incarnate Word.

—*St. Thomas Aquinas, O.P., C.*
Doctor of the Church (+1274)

5.   This Lord (God the Holy Ghost) Who is so singularly with Mary is the Lord Whose most beautiful spouse Mary is. To this Lord, as to this spouse, we can apply the words of Osee: *I will espouse you to Myself in justice, and in judgment, and in mercy, and in commiserations, and I will espouse you to Me in faith; and you shall know that I am the Lord* (Osee 2:19-20). Behold a beautiful spouse, beautiful in justice, and in the judgment of her looks, beautiful in compassion and in mercy in the regard of her neighbors, and beautiful in faith in the sight of God. . . . Of how great sweetness and beauty is that spouse of the Supreme Consoler (the Paraclete)! Because, as St. Augustine says, "Who is this Virgin, so holy that the Holy Spirit deigns to come to her? So beautiful, that God chooses her for His spouse?"

—*St. Bonaventure, O.F.M., Bp. C.*
Doctor of the Church (+1274)

6.   Our God, Jesus, was carried in Mary's bosom by divine dispensation, by the operation of the Holy Spirit.

—*St. Ignatius of Antioch, Bp. M.* (+107)

7.   The Holy Spirit spoke about her through the mouth of the prophets, foretold her by his oracles, painted her picture by means of figures, promised her with the events which preceded her and completed her with the ones that followed her.

—*St. Ildephonsus, Bp. C.* (+667)

8.   The glorious Virgin, Our Lady, never had in her soul the form of any creature whatsoever, nor did she move or do anything on account of it, but her movements were always in and by the Holy Spirit.

—*St. John of the Cross, O. Carm.*
Doctor of the Church (+1591)

9.   Among all Heaven's saints she is the most humble, yet she excels them all in the splendor of her grace and in the fire of her

love. Hence she is called *black but beautiful* (Cant. 1:4), black because of her humility, *for the sun has altered my color* (1:5). Bright sunbeams darken one's complexion. Similarly the sublime light of Divine knowledge produces humility of heart.

—*St. Laurence of Brindisi, O.F.M. Cap.*
Doctor of the Church (+1619)

XII

The Visitation of Our Lady

1.   Vouchsafe, O Lord, we beseech You, to us Your servants the gift of Your heavenly grace; that as the childbearing of the Blessed Virgin was the beginning of our salvation, so from the solemn festival of her Visitation we may obtain an increase of peace. Through Our Lord...

—*A Collect for the Mass of the Visitation*

2.   Blessed and venerable are you, O Virgin Mary: without blemish to your purity you were made the Mother of the Savior.

—*From a Gradual for the Mass of the Visitation.*

3.   *And she entered into the house of Zachary, and saluted Elizabeth. And it came to pass, when Elizabeth heard the greeting of Mary, that the babe in her womb leaped. And Elizabeth was filled with the Holy Spirit, and cried out with a loud voice, saying, Blessed are you among women and blessed is the Fruit of your womb! And how have I deserved that the Mother of my Lord should come to me? For behold, the moment that the sound of your greeting came to my ears, the babe in my womb leaped for joy* (Lk. 1:40-45). See how

great is the power of the words of Our Lady; for no sooner has she pronounced them, than the Holy Ghost is given.

—*St. Bonaventure, O.F.M., Bp. C.*
Doctor of the Church (+1274)

4.   Mary's visit to the household of Zachary has a striking parallel in the Old Testament when the Ark of the Covenant was entrusted to the house of the priest Obededom. King David conducted the Ark to Obededom's house where it remained three months. *And the Lord blessed Obededom and all his household* (2 Kgs. 6:2). He bestowed many gifts upon it. Today, God conducts Mary, the living Ark of the Covenant, to the priestly house of Zachary. She too will remain three months. As a result God blessed this house. The Holy Spirit fills Zachary and Elizabeth (cf. Luke 1:67; 1:41). And John too is filled with the Holy Spirit though still in his mother's womb, leaping and dancing as another David before the Ark of the Lord. Did not Elizabeth say, *The babe in my womb leaped for joy* (Luke 1:44)? But this happened at Mary's word, for she *arose and went with haste into the hill country* after the Son of God had been conceived in her by the Holy Spirit. *And she entered the house of Zachary and saluted Elizabeth. And it came to pass, when Elizabeth heard the greeting of Mary. . .she was filled with the Holy Spirit.*

—*St. Laurence of Brindisi, O.F.M. Cap.*
Doctor of the Church (+1619)

5.   Elizabeth, filled as she was with the Holy Spirit, saw and spoke by Divine inspiration of things past, present and future. . . . She knew, too, the infinite dignity, the present and future glory of the most holy and humble Virgin Mary. Hence in sheer wonder and ecstatic delight she cried out: *Blessed are you among women. . . . How have I deserved that the Mother of my Lord should come to me?. . . Blessed is she who has believed.* Mary's past grace was known to Elizabeth: *Blessed are you;* her present dignity: *the Mother of my Lord;* her future glory: *Blessed is she who*

has believed, because the things promised her by the Lord shall be accomplished.

> —*St. Laurence of Brindisi, O.F.M. Cap.*
> *Doctor of the Church* (+1619)

6.   *Mary, rising up . . . went into the hill country with haste* (Luke 1:39). Rising from the quiet of contemplation to which she was always devoted, and quitting her beloved solitude, she immediately set out for the dwelling of St. Elizabeth; and because *charity bears all things* (1 Cor. 13:7) and cannot support delay, as St. Ambrose remarks on this Gospel, "the Holy Ghost knows not slow undertakings" (*In Luc.* 1), without even reflecting on the arduousness of the journey, this tender Virgin immediately undertook it.

> —*St. Alphonsus Liguori, C.SS.R., Bp. C.*
> *Doctor of the Church* (+1787)

7.   What gentleness and charm in this Visitation made by Mary to her beloved cousin Elizabeth. Each of them is about to bear a child, but for the Virgin Mother this is the most sacred maternity that is possible to imagine on earth. Their two songs mingle and respond in a sweet harmony; "Blessed are you among women" on the one hand, and on the other: "God my Savior has regarded the low estate of his handmaiden: for behold, henceforth all generations will call me blessed."

> —*Pope John XXIII* (+1963)

XIII

Commentary on the Magnificat

1.   From the abundance of her Heart Mary magnifies the

greatness of God's power, holiness and mercy. *He has done great things for me, He Who is mighty and holy is His Name; and for generation upon generation is His mercy, to those who fear Him* (Luke 1:50). God, she declares, is all-powerful, all-holy, and ever merciful. Here this most divine prophetess opens the most profound series of sacred Theology, for Theology treats of God under three aspects: His nature, His power, and His works. And so Mary sings: *My soul magnifies the Lord,* Jehovah, the name of the Divine nature. She speaks of His power: *He Who is mighty has done great things for me, and holy is His Name;* and *for generation upon generation is His mercy.* She speaks of His works: *He has shown might with His arm* by creating, conserving and ruling the world. He has manifested His power by wonderful works: *He has scattered the proud in the conceit of their heart,* for He has scattered forever all the demons who, exalting themselves in the conceit of their heart, had risen up against God. Truly, *He has put down the mighty from their thrones, and has exalted the lowly.* Thus the most Holy Virgin, filled with the Holy Spirit, speaks most sublimely of God.

—*St. Laurence of Brindisi, O.F.M. Cap.
Doctor of the Church* (+1619)

2. To thank God for the graces He has given to Our Lady, her devotees will often say the Magnificat, as the Blessed Mary d'Oignies did, and many other saints. It is the only prayer, the only work, which the Holy Virgin composed, or rather, which Jesus composed in her; for He spoke by her mouth. It is the greatest sacrifice of praise which God ever received from a pure creature in the law of grace. It is, on the one hand, the most humble and grateful, and on the other hand, the most sublime and exalted, of all canticles. There are in that song mysteries so great and hidden that the angels do not know them. The pious and erudite Gerson (Jean le Charlier de Gerson, +1429) employed a great part of his life in composing works upon the most difficult subjects; and yet it was only at the close of his career, and even with trembling, that he undertook to comment

on the Magnificat, so as to crown all his other works. He wrote a folio volume on it, bringing forward many admirable things about that beautiful and divine canticle. Among other things, he says that Our Lady often repeated it herself and especially for thanksgiving after Communion. The learned Benzonius (Rutilio Benzoni, Bp. of Recanati and Loreto, 1587), in explaining the Magnificat relates many miracles wrought by virtue of it, and says that the devils tremble and fly when they hear these words: *He has shown might in His arm; He has scattered the proud in the conceit of their heart.* Those faithful servants of Mary who adopt this devotion ought always greatly to despise, to hate and to eschew the corrupted world.

—*St. Louis-Marie Grignon de Montfort* (+1716)

XIV

The Immaculate Conception

1.   *For she is a vapor of the power of God, and a certain pure emanation of the glory of the Almighty God: and therefore no defiled thing comes into her. For she is the brightness of Eternal Light, and the unspotted mirror of God's Majesty, and the image of His Goodness.*

—*(Wis. 8:25-26)*

2.   We deem indeed only fitting that all the faithful in Christ should give thanks and praise to Almighty God for the marvelous Conception of the Immaculate Virgin, should celebrate and take part in the Masses and other Offices appointed for that purpose, and also strive to gain indulgences and the remission of their sins . . . .

—*Pope Sixtus IV* (+1484)

3.   This devotion and homage toward the Mother of God was

again increased and propagated...so that the universities having adopted this pious belief that she was conceived without sin, already nearly all Catholics have embraced it.

—*Pope Alexander VII* (+1667)

4. In honor of the Holy and Undivided Trinity, to give glory and due honor to the Virgin Mother of God, for the exaltation of the Catholic Faith and the increase of Christian religion, by the authority of Our Lord Jesus Christ, of the blessed Apostles Peter and Paul, and by Our own, We pronounce and define that the doctrine which states that the Most Blessed Virgin Mary was, in the first instant of her conception, by the singular grace and privilege of God, in view of the merits of Jesus Christ the Savior of the human race, preserved immune from all stain of original sin, has been revealed by God and is therefore to be firmly and unswervingly believed by all the faithful. Wherefore if any should presume—which God avert—to think otherwise in their hearts than We have defined, let them know and understand that they stand condemned by their own judgment, that they have made shipwreck of the faith, have fallen away from the unity of the Church, and that in consequence they automatically fall under the canonical penalties if they venture to make known by word or writing or in any other outward way what they think in their hearts.

—*Pope Pius IX* (+1878)

5. If anyone says that man once justified can during his whole life avoid all sins, even venial ones, as the Church holds that the Blessed Virgin did by special privilege of God, let him be anathema.

—*Council of Trent* (1545-1563)

6. The Immaculate Conception of the glorious ever-Virgin Mary, Mother of God, whom on this day Pope Pius IX solemnly

defined to have been by a singular privilege of God preserved free from all stain of original sin.

—*Roman Martyrology, 8 December*

7.   God, by a singular Providence, caused the Most Holy Virgin to be as perfectly pure from the very first moment of her existence, as it was fitting that she should be, who was to be the worthy Mother of God.

—*Greek Menology, 25 March*

8.   Our most holy, immaculate, and most glorious Lady, Mother of God and ever-Virgin Mary.

—*Protoevangelium of St. James (c. A.D. 170)*

9.   All blameless, more to be honored than the Cherubim, incomparably more glorious than the Seraphim.

—*Liturgy of St. James the Apostle*

10. Mary was altogether sinless.

—*Liturgy of St. John Chrysostom*

11. The New Testament shows us that the Son of God was born of a Virgin, and that he is the Christ, the Savior announced by the prophets.

—*St. Irenaeus, Bp. M. (+c. 202)*

12. It was meet that the God of all purity should spring from the greatest purity, from the most pure bosom.

—*St. Irenaeus, Bp. M. (+c. 202)*

13. The only daughter of life, the tabernacle most holy, not made by hands of man, preserved incorrupt, and blessed from the head to the feet.

—*St. Dionysius of Alexandria (+265)*

14. The new Eve, and the Mother of Life.

—St. Athanasius, Bp. C.
Doctor of the Church (+373)

15. Of a truth (O Lord), You and Your Mother are they alone who are in every way wholly fair; for in You, O Lord, there is no spot, in Your Mother no stain.

—St. Ephraem of Edessa
Doctor of the Church (+c. 373)

16. She was as innocent as Eve before her fall, a Virgin most estranged from every stain of sin, more holy than the Seraphim, the sealed fountain of the Holy Ghost, the pure seed of God, ever in body and in mind intact and immaculate.

—St. Ephraem of Edessa
Doctor of the Church (+c. 373)

17. Most holy Lady, Mother of God, alone most pure in soul and body, alone exceeding all perfection of purity...alone made in your entirety the home of all the graces of the Most Holy Spirit, and hence exceeding beyond all compare even the angelic virtues in purity and sanctity of soul and body...my Lady most holy, all-pure, all-immaculate, all-stainless, all-undefiled, all-incorrupt, all-inviolate...spotless robe of Him Who clothes Himself with light as with a garment...flower unfading, purple woven by God, alone most immaculate.

—St. Ephraem of Edessa
Doctor of the Church (+c. 373)

18. She was immaculate, and remote from all stain of sin.

—St. Ephraem of Edessa
Doctor of the Church (+c. 373)

19. Hers was a purity without shadow.

—St. Gregory of Nyssa (+403)

20. Receive me not from Sarah, but from Mary; that it may be an uncorrupted Virgin, a Virgin free by grace from every stain of sin.

—St. Ambrose, Bp. C.
Doctor of the Church (+397)

21. She was a Virgin not in body only, but in mind also; the purity of her thoughts had been defloweded by no evil sug-gestion.... So pure was Blessed Mary that she was chosen to be the Mother of the Lord; God made her whom He had chosen and chose her of whom He would be made.

—St. Ambrose, Bp. C.
Doctor of the Church (+397)

22. He Who formed the first virgin (Eve) without deformity, also made the second Virgin (Mary) without spot or stain.

—St. Amphilochius of Iconium (+c. 400)

23. The immaculate sheep that brought forth Christ the Lamb of God was superior to all things, God alone excepted; she was more beautiful in her nature than the Cherubim, the Seraphim, and the whole host of Angels.... Mary by grace was free from all stain of sin.

—St. Epiphanius, Ab. Bp. C. (+403)

24. *Hail, full of grace* (Luke 1:28). By these words the angel shows that she was altogether excluded from the wrath of the first sentence, and restored to the full grace of blessing.

—St. Augustine, Bp. C.
Doctor of the Church (+430)

25. With the exception therefore of the Holy Virgin Mary, with regard to whom, when sin is in question, I cannot, out of respect of Our Lord, permit of any discussion—for how can we know of any greater grace that could have been bestowed on her for

complete victory over sin, when she merited to conceive and
bring forth Him Who, we all know, had no sin?...

—*St. Augustine, Bp. C.*
Doctor of the Church (+430)

26. *The Most High has sanctified His own tabernacle* (Ps. 45:5).
The Incarnate Word dwelled in a womb which He had created
free from all that might be to His dishonor.

—*St. Proclus, Patriarch of Constantinople* (+446)

27. If any stain or defect had been in her soul, the Lord would
have sought out another Mother for Himself, one perfectly free
from all sin.

—*St. James of Batnae* (+522)

28. The Virgin is therefore called Immaculate, for in nothing
was she corrupt.

—*St. Sophronius* (+c. 650)

29. The serpent never had any access to this paradise.

—*St. John Damascene, Pr. C.*
Doctor of the Church (+c. 749)

30. Our Lord preserved the soul, together with the body, of the
Blessed Virgin in that purity which became her who was to
receive a God in her womb; for as He is holy, He reposes only in
holy places.

—*St. John Damascene, Pr. C.*
Doctor of the Church (+c. 749)

31. The flesh of the Virgin, taken from Adam, did not admit of
the stain of Adam.

—*St. Peter Damian, Bp. C.*
Doctor of the Church (+1072)

32. Mary is that uncorrupted earth which God blessed, and was therefore free from all contagion of sin.

—*St. Bruno, Carth.* (+1101)

33. It was fitting that the conception of the Man Who was the Son of God should be by a Mother most pure. Fitting that the Virgin should be adorned with a purity than which none can be imagined greater below the Divine; the Virgin to whom God the Father decreed to give His only Son, Whom, begotten from His own Heart, equal with Himself, He loved as Himself, that entering the natural order He might become her Son as well as His; whom the Son Himself chose to make His Mother, sub- stance of his substance; of whom the Holy Spirit willed and decreed to effect that of her should be conceived and born Him from Whom He Himself proceeds.

—*St. Anselm, O.S.B. Bp: C.*
Doctor of the Church (+1109)

34. It was becoming that the Blessed Virgin Mary, by whom our shame was to be blotted out, and by whom the devil was to be conquered, should never, even for a moment, have been under his domination.

—*St. Bonaventure, O.F.M., Bp. C.*
Doctor of the Church (+1274)

35. *Let the stars be darkened with the mist thereof. Let it expect light and not see it, nor the rising of the dawning of the day.* (Job 3:9). The dawn, whose rising the night does not see, signifies the Blessed Virgin, whose nativity was not initiated by the night of original sin. For the night which Job cursed, the night in which man was conceived, is original sin . . . . *As the light of the morn- ing, when the sun rises, shines in the morning without clouds* (2 Kgs. 23:4). The light of the morning is the holiness of Mary, by

which the Sun of Justice, Who was about to come from her, irradiated her.

—*St. Bonaventure, O.F.M., Bp. C.*
Doctor of the Church (+1274)

36. Our Sovereign Lady was full of preventing grace for her sanctification: that is, preservative grace against the corruption of original sin.

—*St. Bonaventure, O.F.M., Bp. C.*
Doctor of the Church (+1274)

37. The Holy Ghost, as a very special favor, redeemed and preserved her from original sin by a new kind of sanctification, and this in the very moment of her conception.

—*St. Bonaventure, O.F.M., Bp. C.*
Doctor of the Church (+1274)

38. The Blessed Virgin never committed any actual sin, not even a venial one. Otherwise she would not have been a Mother worthy of Jesus Christ; for the ignominy of the Mother would also have been that of the Son, for He would have had a sinner for His Mother.

—*St. Thomas Aquinas, O.P., C.*
Doctor of the Church (+1274)

39. *You have found grace with God* (Luke 1:31). You have found a singular grace, O most sweet Virgin, that of preservation from original sin.

—*Blessed Raymond Jordano, Ab.* (+1391)

40. It is not to be believed that He, the Son of God, would be born of a Virgin, and take her flesh, were she in the slightest

degree stained with original sin.

—*St. Bernardine of Siena, O.F.M.* (+1444)

41. The third degree of sanctification is that obtained by becoming the Mother of God, and this sanctification consists of entire removal of original sin. This is what took place in the Blessed Virgin: truly God created Mary such, both as to the eminence of her nature and the perfection of grace with which He endowed her, as became Him Who was to be born of her.

—*St. Bernardine of Siena, O.F.M.* (+1444)

42. Before she conceived Him, she was already fit to be the Mother of God.

—*St. Thomas of Villanova, O.S.A.* (+1555)

43. "The one and only daughter of life" (St. Dionysius the Great of Alexandria, 265: *Ep. contra Paul. Sam.*). She is the one and only daughter of life, in contradistinction to others, who being born in sin are daughters of death.

—*St. Alphonsus Liguori, C.SS.R., Bp. C.*
Doctor of the Church (+1787)

44. *As the lily among thorns, so is My love among the daughters* (Cant. 2:2). My daughter, among all My others, you are as a lily in the midst of thorns: for they are all stained with sin, but you were always immaculate, and always My beloved.

—*St. Alphonsus Liguori, C.SS.R., Bp. C.*
Doctor of the Church (+1787)

45. And now if Mary, on account of a single venial sin, which does not deprive a soul of divine grace, would not have been a mother worthy of God, how much more unworthy would she have been had she contracted the guilt of *original* sin, which would have made her an enemy of God and a slave of the

devil... *You are all fair, O my love, and there is not a spot in you* (Cant. 4:7). These words, say St. Ildephonsus and St. Thomas, are properly to be understood of Mary, as Cornelius a Lapide remarks; and St. Bernardine of Siena (*Pro. Fest. V.M.*) and St. Laurence Justinian (*In Nat. B.M.*) assert they are to be understood precisely as applying to her Immaculate Conception; whence Bl. Raymond Jordano addresses her, saying, "You are all fair, O most glorious Virgin, not in part, but wholly; and no stain of mortal, venial or original sin is in you" (*Cont. de V.M.*)

—*St. Alphonsus Liguori, C.SS.R., Bp. C.*
Doctor of the Church (+1787)

46. There is nothing left for me except to die for love of God and of the Virgin Mary, my Lady, my dearly beloved.

Blessed be the Most Holy Sacrament of the Altar and the Immaculate Virgin Mary, who was all holy, without original sin, before she was born of St. Anne.

—*St. Alphonsus Rodriquez, S.J.* (+1617)

47. From her Conception she was anticipated with blessings of sweetness (*prevenisti eam in benedictionibus dulcedinis*) and totally outside the decree of condemnation. She was totally immune to the corruption of the flesh and equally foreign to every stain of sin.

—*St. Laurence Justinian* (+1455)

48. I, John Berchmans, most unworthy son of the Society of Jesus, standing before you, O Mary, and before your Son, whom I believe and profess to be present in this august Sacrament of the Eucharist, do publicly declare that I shall always and forever—except the Church should otherwise decide—hold and defend your Immaculate Conception. And in witness thereof, I sign this with my own blood and seal it with the seal of the Society of Jesus, on the year of Our Lord, 1620.

—*St. John Berchmans, S.J.* (+1621)

49. You, O sweetest Virgin Mary, my Mother!, you are the patroness and advocate of my holiness, my health and my studies! O Mary, most holy Mother of God and Immaculate Virgin, receive me from henceforth and forever as your slave, help me in all my actions, and do not forsake me at the hour of my death.

—*St. John Berchmans, S.J.* (+1621)

50. She who had been sanctified in the womb of her mother, and freed from every contamination of original sin, shows in her exterior the fullness of grace that she had received in her soul.

—*St. Laurence Justinian* (+1455)

51. It is certain that the Word loved her when she was yet in the womb of her mother and chose her for his Mother, for she has been forestalled with superabundant blessings and destined for the Magisterium of the Holy Ghost.

—*St. Laurence Justinian* (+1455)

XV

Blessed Mary, Ever-Virgin

1.   You are happy, O Virgin Mary, who has borne the Creator: you have engendered Him Who created you, yet remaining always a Virgin.

—*An Office for the Maternity of Our Lady*

2.   Blessed are you, O Virgin Mary, who did bear the Lord, the Creator of the world. You did bring forth Him Who made you and remain a Virgin forever (*et in aeternum permanes Virgo*)

—*A Response from Lesson II of Matins Officium Parvum B.V.M.*

3. But O Virgin Lady, Immaculate Mother of God, my glorious Lady, my benefactress, higher than the heavens, far more pure than the sun in its rays of shining splendor . . . the rod of Aaron that budded, truly have you appeared as a stem whose flower is your true Son, our Christ, my God and my Maker; you did bear according to the flesh God and the Word, did preserve your virginity before His birth, did remain a virgin after His birth, and we have been reconciled to God by Christ your Son.

—St. Ephraem of Edessa
Doctor of the Church (+c. 373)

4. Of Him Who is God and Man are you the Mother, Virgin before (His) birth, Virgin in birth, and Virgin after birth.

—St. Cyril of Jerusalem
Doctor of the Church (+386)

5. So great was her grace, that not only it preserved her own virginity, but conferred that admirable gift of purity on those who beheld her.

—St. Ambrose, Bp. C.
Doctor of the Church (+397)

6. Was there ever a person who in speaking of Mary would, when questioned, refuse to add at once the epithet "Virgin"? For the proofs of her virtue shine out in the conjunction of those very terms. . . . She is termed "Holy Mary," a title that will never be changed, for she *ever remains inviolate*.

—St. Epiphanius, Ab. Bp. C. (+403)

7. We believe that God was born of a virgin because we read it; because we do not read it we do not believe that Mary wedded again after the birth of her Child. Nor do we say this be-

cause we would condemn marriage; for surely virginity itself is the fruit of marriage.

—*St. Jerome, Pr. C.*
Doctor of the Church (+420)

8. *My sister, My spouse, is a garden enclosed, a fountain sealed up* (Cant. 4:12). Mary was this enclosed garden and sealed fountain, into which no guile could enter, against which no fraud of the enemy could prevail, and who always was holy in mind and body.

—*St. Sophronius* (+c. 640)

9. A privilege of Mary was that she alone was a mother and at the same time an inviolable virgin. St. Bernard, praising this privilege, says: "Mary chose for herself the better part." Clearly the better, because conjugal fecundity, or fecund virginity. The privilege of Mary will not be given to another, because it will not be taken away from her.

—*St. Bonaventure, O.F.M., Bp. C.*
Doctor of the Church (+1274)

10. In chastity you must imitate the Virgin of virgins, putting yourselves under her protection. The same also in obedience, obey her, who was always so obedient to St. Joseph, her virginal spouse.

—*St. Joachima Vedruna de Mas* (+1854)

11. According to the flesh, Our Lord Jesus Christ, was born from the stock of David; but if we look at the will and the power of God, He is the Son of God, truly born of a virgin.

—*St. Ignatius of Antioch, Bp. M.* (+107)

12. If I seek the Mother, I see that she is a Virgin. If I seek the Virgin, I see that she is a Mother. And this virginity is ever incorrupt, ever perfect, ever inviolate.

—*St. Ildephonsus, Bp. C.* (+667)

13. God allowed the Blessed Virgin to suffer so that she would merit more.

> —*St. John of the Cross, O. Carm.*
> *Doctor of the Church* (+1591)

14. The chief remedy against the Devil is to have recourse to the Virgin Mary.

> —*St. John of Avila* (+1569)

15. Behold Holy Mary in glory, the Mother of the Lord, exuberant with joy. She is the peak and model of virginity, she the mother of every holy and incorrupt thing. She has begotten you while remaining intact; painlessly she gave birth to you by her teachings, and conceived your Bridegroom Jesus keeping her virginity.

> —*St. Leander, Bp. C.* (+600)

XVI

Mary's Divine Maternity

1. O God, Who did will that your Word should take flesh, at the message of an angel, in the womb of the Blessed Virgin Mary: grant unto us your suppliants that we who believe her to be indeed the Mother of God may be aided by her intercession with you. Through the same Our Lord...

> —*A Collect for the Feast of the*
> *Maternity B.V.M., 11 October*

2. Your Maternity, O Mother of God and Virgin, has announced joy to the whole world: because out of you is arisen the Sun of Justice, Christ our God.

> —*An Antiphon to Magnificat*
> *Second Vespers of Maternity B.V.M.*

3.   Through the conception of the Divine Word, Mary has become for us the heaven that enclosed the Divinity in the narrow arch of her womb for the purpose of exalting mortals to the great dignity of kinship of God!

> —*St. Ephraem of Edessa*
> *Doctor of the Church (+c. 373)*

4.   The nobility of the Child was in the virginity which brought Him forth, and the nobility of the parent was in the Divinity of the Child.

> —*St. Augustine, Bp. C.*
> *Doctor of the Church (+430)*

5.   Mary, the Virgin Mother, brings forth today the Author of grace. She is the Mother and Sovereign of the universe; she remains a Virgin as she gives birth today to her Son. The sun begets the Sun; the creature gives birth to the Creator. She is His child and she is His Mother. Mary was chosen as Mother, predestined before all creatures, filled with all grace, all virtue, all holiness, to the end that of a Mother most pure might be born the Son infinitely pure. And as in Heaven the Son has a Father immortal and eternal, so on earth the Son, according to the flesh, is like the Mother. In Heaven He is eternal and immense with the Father; on earth, like the Mother, He is in time and full of meekness. In Heaven He is the image of the Father; on earth He is the likeness of His Mother.

> —*St. Augustine, Bp. C.*
> *Doctor of the Church (+430)*

6.   Hail, Mother and Virgin, living and immortal tabernacle of God, the world's treasure and light, ornament of virgins, support of true faith, firm foundation of every church. You who gave birth to God, and carried under your pure Heart Him Whom space cannot contain. You through whom the Holy Trinity is praised and worshipped, and through whom the holy

Cross is venerated in the whole world. . . . Who can worthily praise you who are above all praise?

> —*St. Cyril of Alexandria, Bp. C.*
> *Doctor of the Church* (+444)

7.   *Blessed is the Fruit of your womb* (Luke 1:43). By the entrance of His only-begotten Son, the Lord consecrated by the grace of the Holy Ghost the temple of the virginal womb. And our earth will give its fruit, because the same Virgin, who had her body from the earth, brought forth a Son, co-equal indeed in divinity with God the Father, but in the reality of His flesh consubstantial with *her.*

> —*St. Bede the Venerable, O.S.B.*
> *Doctor of the Church* (+735)

8.   Well is He called the Fruit of salvation, without Whom we have no salvation, according to that word: *There is no salvation in any other.* And St. Anselm says: "There is no salvation except Him Whom you, O Virgin, have brought forth." You, therefore, O Mary, are truly the tree of salvation, who has borne for the world the Fruit of salvation.

> —*St. Bonaventure, O.F.M., Bp. C.*
> *Doctor of the Church* (+1274)

9.   *Woe to them who are with child and bring forth in those days* (Mt. 24:19). Oh, how far from this woe was Mary when she conceived and brought forth, as St. Augustine testifies saying, "How blessed is that Mother who without stain conceived Purity, and without pain brought forth Healing."

> —*St. Bonaventure, O.F.M., Bp. C.*
> *Doctor of the Church* (+1274)

10. Jesus is the son of Mary and the son of God.

> —*St. Ignatius of Antioch, Bp. M.* (+107)

11. The two sons of Mary are the God-Man, in His Divinity, and man, in his humanity. Mary is the Mother of one in the body, of the other in the spirit. Wherefore St. Bernard says: "You are the Mother of the King, you are the Mother of the exile; you are the Mother of God the Judge, and you are the Mother of God and of man; as you are the Mother of both, you can not bear discord between your two sons."

—*St. Bonaventure, O.F.M., Bp. C.*
Doctor of the Church (+1274)

12. This fair lovely word *Mother*, it is so sweet and kind itself that it may not verily be said of any but of Him, and to her that is very Mother of Him and of all. To the property of Motherhood belongs kind love, wisdom and knowing; and it is good: for though it be so that our bodily forthbringing be but little, low, and simple in regard of our ghostly forthbringing, yet it is He that does it in the creatures by whom that it is done. The kind, loving Mother that understands and knows the need of her Child, she keeping Him full tenderly, and the kind and condition of Motherhood will. And as He increases in age, she changes her working, but not her love.

—*Blessed Dame Julian of Norwich, Recluse* (+c. 1415)

XVII

Mother of God

1.   Hail, O Mary, Mother of God, Virgin and Mother!
        Morning Star, perfect vessel.
      Hail, O Mary, Mother of God! holy temple in which God
        Himself was conceived.
      Hail, O Mary, Mother of God! chaste and pure dove.
      Hail, O Mary, Mother of God! ever-effulgent light; from
        you proceeds the Sun of Justice.

Hail, O Mary, Mother of God! you did enclose in your
sacred womb the One Who cannot be encompassed.

Hail, O Mary, Mother of God! With the shepherds we sing
the praise of God, and with the angels the song of
thanksgiving: Glory to God in the highest and peace on
earth to men of good will.

Hail, O Mary, Mother of God! Through you came to us the
Conqueror and triumphant Vanquisher of hell.

Hail, O Mary, Mother of God! Through you blossoms the
splendor of the Resurrection.

Hail, O Mary, Mother of God! You have saved every
faithful Christian.

Hail, O Mary, Mother of God! Who can praise you
worthily, O glorious Virgin Mary?

—*St. Cyril of Alexandria, Bp. C.*
Doctor of the Church (+444)

2.   In order to be a devoted servant of the Father, I faithfully
desire to be the servant of the Mother.

—*St. Ildephonsus, Bp. C. (+667)*

3.   The Virgin Mary who at the message of the angel received
the Word of God in her heart and in her body and gave life to
the world, is acknowledged and honored as being truly the
Mother of God and the Redeemer. Redeemed in a more exalted
fashion, by reason of the merits of her Son and united to him by
a close and indissoluble tie, she is endowed with the high office
and dignity of the Mother of the Son of God, and therefore she
is also the beloved daughter of the Father and the temple of the
Holy Spirit.

—*Vatican II, Chapter VIII on Our Lady in the*
Dogmatic Constitution on the Church

4.   Wherefore this sacred synod, while expounding the doctrine on the Church in which the divine Redeemer brings about
our salvation, intends to set forth painstakingly both the role of

the Blessed Virgin in the mystery of the Incarnate Word and the Mystical Body and the duties of the redeemed towards the Mother of God, who is Mother of Christ and mother of men and most of all those who belive.

—*Vatican II*

5.   Contemplate the virginity and the poverty of Mary who was so rich in the eyes of God that she deserved to be the Mother of Christ, and so poor in material goods that at the point of delivery she did not even have a woman to help her. Her abode was so dilapidated that she had to ask a crib to serve for a cradle.

—*St. Leander, Bp. C.* (+600)

6.   What greater prodigy could the world behold, than a woman become the Mother of God, and a God clothed in human flesh? Mary, by her humility, became the Mother of her Creator. The Creator, in His goodness, became the Son of His own creature.

—*St. Alphonsus Liguori, C.SS.R., Bp. C.*
Doctor of the Church (+1787)

7.   She is the mighty Mother of the Almighty.

—*Pope Leo XIII* (+1903)

8.   If anyone shall say that the holy, glorious and ever-Virgin Mary was only in a certain sense and not most truly the Mother of God, or that she was so in some merely relative way as though it were simply a man that was born and not the Word of God that became incarnate and was born of her, or shall refer, as some do, the birth of the man to God the Word only in the sense that the Word was with the man when he was born; or if they calumniate the Holy Synod of Chalcedon, which calls the Virgin the Mother of God, by putting on those words the interpretation foisted on them by the detestable Theodore,

calling her for example, the mother of the man or the "Christo-tokos," that is the "mother of Christ," as though Christ were not God, and thus refuse to acknowledge her to be—as she is—really and truly the very Mother of God since He Who before the ages was God, the Word born of the Father, did in these last days take flesh of her and of her was born, as the Holy Synod of Chalcedon has devoutly acknowledged, let such a man be anathema.

—*Second Council of Constantinople (5th Ecumenical)*

9. In adherence to the Synodical Letters written by the blessed Cyril against the impious Nestorius and to those written to the Bishops of the East, following, too, in the footsteps of the five Holy and Universal Synods and of the holy and approved Fathers, we unanimously define that Our Lord Jesus Christ is to be acknowledged as our true God, one from the holy and consubstantial Trinity which is the origin of life, perfect in Godhead, the same, too, perfect in human nature, truly God and truly man, the same made of a rational soul and a body; consubstantial with the Father according to Godhead, consubstantial with us according to human nature, *in all things like unto us, save without sin* (Heb. 4:15); according to Godhead begotten of the Father before the ages, but also in these last days the same conceived, for us men and for our salvation, of the Holy Spirit and the Virgin Mary who was really and truly the Mother of God according to His human nature, one and the same to be acknowledged as Christ, Only-begotten Son of God, in two natures, not commingled, not changed into one another, inseparable one from the other yet indivisible; the differences between these two natures in no sense removed by reason of their union but rather the peculiar properties of each preserved, though concurring to form one Person and one subsistence; one and the same Only-begotten Son of God, the Word, the Lord Jesus Christ, not divided nor shared between two persons, according as the Prophets of old and Our Lord Jesus Christ

Himself taught us and the Creed of the Holy Fathers has handed down to us.

—*Third Council of Constantinople*
(6th General) A.D. 680-681

10. If anyone does not believe that Holy Mary is the Mother of God, such an one is a stranger to the Godhead. If anyone shall say that (Christ) passed through the Virgin as through a channel and was not formed in her both in divine and human fashion —*divine* because without a husband's cooperation, *human* because conceived in accordance with human law—such an one too is an atheist. If anyone shall say that a man was made, and that afterwards God entered into him—he renders himself liable to damnation.

—*St. Gregory Nazianzen*
Doctor of the Church (+390)

11. If anyone should not confess that Emmanuel is truly God, and that in consequence the Blessed Virgin is the Mother of God—for she brought forth according to the flesh the Word of God made flesh—let him be anathema.

—*St. Cyril's "Anathemas," can. 1 of the*
(Third Ecumenical) Council of Ephesus, A.D. 431

12. You, O Mary, have given birth to the Creator, in you began the Origin of all creation; in your womb God dwelt.

—*St. Peter Chrysologus, Bp. C.*
Doctor of the Church (+c. 450)

13. Let Nestorius be filled with shame and lay his hand on his lips. This Child is God. How then shall she who bore Him not be God's Mother? But if anyone refuses to acknowledge her as Mother of God, such an one is far removed from the Godhead. These are not my words, though it is I who use them, for I

inherited these glorious teachings from Gregory the Theologian.

—*St. John Damascene, Pr. C.*
Doctor of the Church (+c. 749)

14. When we say that Mary is the Mother of God, this alone transcends every greatness that can be named or imagined after that of God.

—*St. Anselm, O.S.B., Bp. C.*
Doctor of the Church (+1109)

15. To be the Mother of God is the greatest grace which can be conferred on a creature. It is such that God could make a greater world, a greater Heaven, but He cannot exalt a creature more than by making her His Mother.

—*St. Bonaventure, O.F.M., Bp. C.*
Doctor of the Church (+1274)

16. The Blessed Virgin, by becoming the Mother of God, received a kind of infinite dignity because God is infinite; this dignity therefore is such a reality that a better is not possible, just as nothing can be better than God.

—*St. Thomas Aquinas, O.P., C.*
Doctor of the Church (+1274)

17. What greater prodigy could the world behold than a woman become the Mother of God, and a God clothed in human flesh? Mary by her humility, became the Mother of her Creator. The Creator, in His goodness, became the Son of His own creature.

—*St. Alphonsus Liguori, C.SS.R., Bp. C.*
Doctor of the Church (+1787)

18. *From a letter to St. Germanus, Patriarch of Constantinople, on the veneration of sacred images:*

"We venerate also the holy image of Our Lady, the truly most pure Mother of God, whose face, as it is written, will entreat all the rich among the people, with their prayers."

—*Pope St. Gregory II* (+731)

19. When we pray before an image of the Lord's Holy Mother, we say: Most Holy Mother of God, Mother of Our Lord, intercede before your Son, our true God, so that he may save our souls.

—*Pope St. Gregory II* (+731)

XVIII

Daughter, Mother and Spouse of God

1. *The Lord is with you* (Luke 1:28). The Father is with you, because He made His Son yours; the Son is with you, Who, in order to work in you an admirable secret, in a wonderful manner unlocked the secret room of generation, and kept for you the seal of virginity; the Holy Ghost is with you, Who together with the Father sanctified your womb.

—*St. Bernard of Clairvaux, Cist.*
Doctor of the Church (+1153)

2. Holy Virgin Mary, there is none like you born in the world among women. O daughter and handmaid of the most High King, the heavenly Father! Mother of our Most High Lord Jesus Christ! Spouse of the Holy Ghost! Pray for us...to your most holy Son, our Lord and Master.

—*St. Francis of Assisi, C.* (+1226)

3. She became in a wonderful and singular manner the daughter of the Lord, the mother of the Lord, the spouse of the

Lord, and the handmaid of the Lord. If we wish to describe her relation to each Divine Person, we can say that the Lord Who is with Mary is the Lord and Father, the Lord and Son, the Lord and Holy Ghost, the Lord Who is triune and one. He is the Father and Lord, of Whom Mary is the most noble daughter. He is the Son and Lord, of Whom Mary is the most worthy Mother; He is the Holy Ghost and Lord, of Whom Mary is the most just spouse; He is the Lord Triune and One of Whom Mary is the most submissive handmaid. Mary certainly is the Daughter of the Most High Trinity, the Mother of the Most High Truth, the Spouse of the Most High Goodness, the Handmaid of the Most High Trinity.

—*St. Bonaventure, O.F.M., Bp. C.*
Doctor of the Church (+1274)

4. How could she but be powerful, she who merits the triple title: *Domini Filia, Domini Mater, Domini Sponsa*, Daughter of God, Mother of God, Spouse of God.

—*St. Bonaventure, O.F.M., Bp. C.*
Doctor of the Church (+1274)

5. I venerate you with all my heart, O Virgin most holy, above all Angels and Saints in paradise, as the Daughter of the Eternal Father, and to you I consecrate my soul with all its powers. Hail Mary, etc.

I venerate you with all my heart, O Virgin most holy, above all Angels and Saints in paradise, as the Mother of the only-begotten Son, and to you I consecrate my body with all its senses. Hail Mary, etc.

I venerate you with all my heart, O Virgin most holy, above all Angels and Saints in paradise, as the beloved Spouse of the Spirit of God, and to you I consecrate my heart and all its affections, imploring you to obtain for me from the Most Holy Trinity all the means of salvation. Hail Mary, etc.

—*Pope Leo XII* (+1829)

6.   Albeit the work of three,
                         in One it is perfected;
                         the Word becomes incarnate
                         in the womb of Blessed Mary.
                         And He who had but Father,
                         has now a Mother too...
                         Therefore the Son of God
                         and Son of Man he is called.

                              —*St. John of the Cross, O. Carm.*
                               Doctor of the Church (+1591)

XIX

Purification—Presentation of Jesus

1.   The Virgin was not subject to the law of purification in
Deuteronomy: since without human generation she became
Emmanuel's Mother pure and holy and undefiled; and, having
become Mother, remained still a Virgin.

                              —*St. Basil the Great, Bp. C.*
                               Doctor of the Church (+379)

2.   On this day the Virgin Mother brings the Lord of the
Temple into the Temple of the Lord; Joseph presents to the
Lord a Son, Who is not his own but the Blessed Son of that
Lord Himself, and in Whom He is well pleased; Simeon, the
just man, confesses Him for Whom he had been so long wait-
ing; Anna, too, the widow, confesses Him. The Procession of
this solemnity was first made by these four, which afterwards
was to be made, to the joy of the whole earth, in every place and
by every nation.

                              —*St. Bernard of Clairvaux, Cist.*
                               Doctor of the Church (+1153)

3. *And he (Simeon) said to Mary His Mother: Behold this Child is set for the fall and for the resurrection of many in Israel and for a sign which shall be contradicted and your own soul a sword shall pierce.* The sword signifies the bitter passion and death of her Son. The material sword cannot kill or wound the soul, so the sharp Passion of Christ, although by compassion it pierced the soul of Mary, never dealt it a mortal wound.

—*St. Bonaventure, O.F.M., Bp. C.
Doctor of the Church* (+1274)

4. St. Simeon received a promise from God that he should not die until he had seen the Messias (Luke 2:26). But this grace he received through Mary, for it was in her arms that he found the Savior. Hence, he who desires to find Jesus, will not find Him otherwise than by Mary.

—*St. Alphonsus Liguori, C.SS.R., Bp. C.
Doctor of the Church* (+1787)

5. But the Blessed Virgin did not offer Him as other mothers offered their sons. Others also offered them to God, but they knew that this oblation was simply a legal ceremony, and that by redeeming them they made them their own, without a fear of having again to offer them to death. Mary really offered her Son to death, and knew for certain that the sacrifice of the life of Jesus which she then made was one day to be actually consummated on the Altar of the Cross; so that Mary, by offering the life of her Son, came, in consequence of the love she bore this Son, really to sacrifice her own entire self to God. . . . Although from the moment she became the Mother of Jesus, Mary consented to His death, yet God willed that on this day she should make a solemn sacrifice of herself, by offering her Son to Him in the Temple, sacrificing His precious life to Divine Justice. Hence St. Epiphanius (+403) calls her a "priest" (*Virginam appello velut sacerdotem [Hom. in Laud. S.M.]*). And now we begin to see how much this sacrifice cost her, and what

heroic virtues she had to practice when she herself subscribed the sentence by which her beloved Jesus was condemned to death.

—*St. Alphonsus Liguori, C.SS.R., Bp. C.*
Doctor of the Church (+1787)

6.   *And your own soul a sword shall pierce* (Luke 2:35). Compassion alone for the sufferings of this most beloved Son was the sword of sorrow which was to pierce the Heart of the Mother, as St. Simeon exactly foretold. Already the most Blessed Virgin, as St. Simeon says, was enlightened by the Sacred Scriptures and knew the sufferings that the Redeemer was to endure.... Mary, I say, already knew all these torments that her Son was to endure, but in the words addressed to her by St. Simeon, all the minute circumstances of the sufferings, internal and external, that were to torment her Jesus in His Passion, were made known to her, as Our Lord revealed to St. Teresa.

—*St. Alphonsus Liguori, C.SS.R., Bp. C.*
Doctor of the Church (+1787)

XX

Mother of Divine Grace

1.   O you who are full of grace, all creation rejoices in you! The hierarchies of the angels and the race of men rejoice. O sanctified temple and rational paradise, virginal glory, of whom God took flesh! He Who is God before all ages, became a child. Your womb He made His throne, and your lap He made greater than the heavens. Indeed all creation exults in you. Glory be to you!

—From the *Byzantine Liturgy of St. Basil*

2.   Happy she who has become for all creation the fountain that pours out all good things! From her has shone light for all creatures.

—*St. Ephraem of Edessa*
Doctor of the Church (+c. 373)

3.   On others grace was bestowed in measure; but the whole fullness was poured into Mary.

—*St. Jerome, Pr. C.*
Doctor of the Church (+420)

4.   She is a boundless ocean, an unfathomable sea, a profound abyss of grace.

—*St. Sophronius, C.* (+c. 640)

5.   I am the city of refuge, says Our Lady, for all those who have recourse to me. Come, then, to me, my children; for from me you will obtain graces, and these in greater abundance than you can possibly imagine.

—*St. John Damascene, Pr. C.*
Doctor of the Church (+c. 749)

6.   Mary is the Mother of all graces.

—*St. Anselm, O.S.B., Bp. C.*
Doctor of the Church (+1109)

7.   By you we have access to your Son, O blessed finder of grace, Mother of Life, Mother of Salvation, that by you He may receive us, Who by you was given to us.

—*St. Bernard of Clairvaux, Cist.*
Doctor of the Church (+1153)

8.   To venerate the Madonna aids us in living our faith in "spirit and in truth"; and helps us to follow the sublime and

human example of Mary; and in doing so, we can ask her heavenly assistance in our daily needs as well as in the greater needs of the world today.

The plan of Providence, that is to say, the Divine action in human affairs, avails itself of prayer for success; and so much the more if to our prayers there is added the more worthy intercession of Mary, the Mother of our Savior.

—*Pope Paul VI* (+1978)

9.   Have recourse to the most pure Virgin Mary, our Mother, who is the Treasurer of all the "Lord's divine graces."

—*St. Joachima Vedruna de Mas* (+1854)

10. She is a full aqueduct, that others may receive of her plenitude.... But why did St. Gabriel, having found the divine Mother already full of grace, according to his salutation, *Hail, full of grace!* afterward say, that the Holy Ghost would come upon her to fill her still more with grace? If she was already full of grace, what more could the coming of the Divine Spirit effect? Mary was already full of grace; but the Holy Ghost filled her to overflowing, *for our good*, that from her superabundance we miserable creatures might be provided.

—*St. Bernard of Clairvaux, Cist.*
Doctor of the Church (+1153)

11. You, O Lady, teach us to hope for far greater graces than we deserve, since you never cease to dispense graces far beyond our merits.

—*St. Hildebert of Fontanelle, Ab.* (+752)

12. No other created being can obtain for us so many and such eminent graces from God as His Mother.

—*St. William of Paris* (+1202)

13. *A gracious woman shall find glory* (Prov. 11:16). O truly

happy finder, Mary, who is so great in this world, so great in Heaven! No pure creature found such grace in this world, such glory in Heaven. And certainly she found both grace and glory with the Lord, for as it is said in the Psalm, *The Lord will give grace and glory* (Ps. 83:12).

—St. Bonaventure, O.F.M., Bp. C.
Doctor of the Church (+1274)

14. *Grace upon grace has a chaste and holy woman* (Ecclus. 26:19). The woman chaste above all women is Mary, the woman holy above all women, in whom is grace above grace, the grace of glory above the grace of the way, the grace of rewards in Heaven above, the grace of merits in this world.

—St. Bonaventure, O.F.M., Bp. C.
Doctor of the Church (+1274)

15. *With me are riches and glory, glorious riches and justice. That I may enrich them that love me, and may fill their treasures* (Prov. 8:18, 21). We ought all to keep our eyes constantly fixed on Mary's hands, that through them we may receive the graces that we desire.

—St. Bonaventure, O.F.M., Bp. C.
Doctor of the Church (+1274)

16. *Let us go, therefore, with confidence to the throne of grace, that we may obtain mercy, and find grace in seasonable aid* (Heb. 4:16). The throne of grace is the Blessed Virgin Mary.

—St. Albertus Magnus, O.P., Pr. C.
Doctor of the Church (+1280)

17. My child, let us honor and venerate the Holy Virgin, for there is no more excellent means to obtain graces from God than to seek them through Mary, because her Divine Son cannot refuse her anything.

—St. Philip Neri, (+1595)

18. During her life on earth, Mary received such a plenitude of graces and merits that it would be easier to count the stars of the firmament, the drops of the ocean, and the sands of the sea-shore, than number her merits and graces.

—*St. Louis-Marie Grignon de Montfort* (+1716)

XXI

At the Foot of the Cross

1.   The Doctors of the Church are unanimous in affirming that it was by a special design of Divine Providence that the Blessed Virgin Mary, who appears so little in the public life of Jesus, was near Him on His way to death and at His Crucifixion. Nay, the Passion and Death of her Son were in a certain sense her Passion and Death, for she utterly surrendered her motherly rights over Jesus.

—*Pope Benedict* XV (+1922)

2.   The lance which opened His side (John 19:34) passed through the soul of the Blessed Virgin, which could never leave her Son's Heart.

—*St. Bernard of Clairvaux, Cist.*
Doctor of the Church (+1153)

3.   Those wounds which were scattered over the body of Our Lord were all united in the single Heart of Mary.

—*St. Bonaventure, O.F.M., Bp. C.*
Doctor of the Church (+1274)

4.   O Lady, tell me, where did you stand? Was it only at the foot of the Cross? Ah, much more than this, you were on the

Cross itself, crucified with your Son.

—*St. Bonaventure, O.F.M., Bp. C.*
Doctor of the Church (+1274)

5.　When she saw the love the Eternal Father towards men to be so great that, in order to save them, He willed the death of His Son; and, on the other hand, seeing the love of the Son in wishing to die for us: in order to conform herself who was always and in all things united to the will of God to this excessive love of both the Father and the Son towards the human race, she also with her entire will offered, and consented to, the death of her Son, in order that we might be saved.

—*St. Bonaventure, O.F.M., Bp. C.*
Doctor of the Church (+1274)

6.　As all the world is under obligation to Jesus for his Passion, so also are we under obligation to Our Lady for her compassion.

—*St. Albertus Magnus, O.P., Pr. C.*
Doctor of the Church (+1280)

7.　While grieving she rejoiced, that a sacrifice was offered for the Redemption of all, by which He Who was angry was appeased.

—*Blessed Simon of Cassia, O.S.A.*
(Simeone Fidati, +1348)

8.　How was your maternal Heart ever able to support this infinite sorrow? Blessed be that Heart compared to whose sorrow everything that ever was uttered of a heart's sorrow is only as a dream to the reality.

—*Blessed Henry Suso, O.P.* (+1365)

9.　The Passion of Christ was as it were mirrored in the Heart of the Virgin, in which might be seen, faithfully reflected, the spitting, the blows and wounds, and all that He suffered.

—*St. Laurence Justinian* (+1455)

10. On these words of the Gospel, *there stood by the Cross of Jesus His Mother* (John 19:25) St. Antoninus says, "Mary stood, supported by her faith, which she retained firm in the divinity of Christ." And for this reason it is, the Saint adds, that in the Office of *Tenebrae* only one candle is left lighted. St. Leo the Great (+461), on this subject, applies to Our Blessed Lady the words of Proverbs (31:18), *Her lamp shall not be put out in the night.*

—*St. Alphonsus Liguori, C.SS.R., Bp. C. Doctor of the Church* (+1787)

11. She gave Him to us a thousand and a thousand times, during the three hours preceding His death, and which she spent at the foot of the Cross; for during the whole of that time she unceasingly offered, with the extreme of sorrow and the extreme of love, the life of her Son in our behalf, and this with such constancy, that St. Anselm (Abp. of Canterbury, +1109) and St. Antoninus (O.P., Abp. of Florence, +1459) say, that if executioners had been wanting she herself would have crucified Him, in order to obey the Eternal Father Who willed His death for our salvation. If Abraham had such fortitude as to be ready to sacrifice with his own hands the life of his son, with far greater fortitude would Mary (far more holy and obedient than Abraham) have sacrificed the life of hers.

—*St. Alphonsus Liguori, C.SS.R., Bp. C. Doctor of the Church* (+1787)

12. *Then the disciples all leaving Him, fled* (Mt. 26:56). . . . *Now there stood by the Cross of Jesus His Mother* (John 19:25). His loving Mother did not abandon Him; she remained with Him until He expired. . .she did not go to a distance, but drew nearer to the Cross, the hard bed on which Jesus Christ had to die. Mary, who stood by its side, never turned her eyes from Him;

she beheld Him...suspended by those three iron hooks.

—*St. Alphonsus Liguori, C.SS.R., Bp. C.*
Doctor of the Church (+1787)

13. O Most Holy Virgin, who were constituted Mother of sinners at the foot of the Cross, give us your holy blessing, so that, sheltered under your holy mantle, we may follow in your footsteps, and be truly meek and humble of heart.

—*St. Joachima Vedruna de Mas* (+1854)

14. Following the poverty and humility of the Beloved Son of God and of the glorious Virgin His Mother, let our nuns always observe the Holy Poverty that they vowed to God.

—*St. Clare of Assisi, V.* (+1253)

15. Meditate assiduously on the mysteries of the Passion and on the Sorrows of the Most Holy Mother of God at the foot of the Cross. Watch and pray at all times.

—*St. Clare of Assisi, V.* (+1253)

16. It was the most Holy Virgin who first thought of this pious devotion of the Way of the Cross. She herself practiced it and handed it down to her faithful servants. It was what she said herself to St. Bridget. "Know, my daughter," she told her, "that during all the time I lived after the Ascension of my Divine Son, I visited every day those holy places where He suffered, where He died, and where He showed forth His mercies." Now, I ask you, as good Christians, does not this one motive, this knowledge that the Way of the Cross was invented, not by any one saint or other, but by the august Mother of God—does not this motive alone, I ask, suffice to win your hearts and enkindle your fervor? Can you not take a resolution to practice it as often as possible, seeing that the Blessed Virgin practiced it every day? Let us add that Adricomius (Christian Kruik van Adrichem, +1585), a writer of great authority, not merely attributes to the

Blessed Virgin the origin of the Way of the Cross (*Jerusalem sicut Christi tempore floruit*, pub. 1584), but asserts, moreover, that it is this pious practice which has given birth in the Church to the custom of having processions, and always with the Cross at the head. He bases his assertion on a pious and ancient tradition; and, indeed, there are many things in the Church which we know only by tradition handed down from father to son.

—*St. Leonard of Port Maurice, O.F.M.* (+1751)

17. Just as the Father gave us the great gift of his Son to be our Redeemer, so also the Son gives us the great gift of his Blessed Mother to be our Advocate. When he said to John at the foot of the Cross: "Behold your Mother!" he said it to him representing all Christians.

—*St. John of Avila* (+1569)

XXII

Queen of Martyrs

1. As the sun surpasses all the stars in lustre, so the sorrows of Mary surpass all the tortures of the martyrs.

—*St. Basil the Great, Bp. C.*
Doctor of the Church (+379)

2. That Mary was a true martyr cannot be doubted, as Denys the Carthusian, Pelbart, Catharinus and others prove; for it is an undoubted opinion that suffering sufficient to cause death is martyrdom, even though death does not ensue from it. St. John the Evangelist is revered as a martyr, though he did not die in the caldron of boiling oil, but came out more vigorous than he went in. St. Thomas says "that to have the glory of martyrdom, it is sufficient to exercise obedience in its highest degree, that is to say, to be obedient unto death." "Mary was a martyr," says

St. Bernard, "not by the sword of the executioner, but by the bitter sorrow of heart."

—*St. Alphonsus Liguori, C.SS.R., Bp. C.*
Doctor of the Church (+1787)

3.   O marvelous patience and meekness of Mary, who was not only most patient while her Son was crucified in her presence, but also before the crucifixion, when her Son was reviled, as it is said in the Gospel of Mark, *Is not this the Son of the carpenter and of Mary?* and a little further on, *And they were scandalized in Him.*

—*St. Jerome, Pr. C.*
Doctor of the Church (+420)

4.   *O all you that pass by the way, attend and see if there be any sorrow like to my sorrow* (Lam. 1:12). To say that Mary's sorrows were greater than all the torments of the martyrs united, were to say too little.

—*St. Ildephonsus, Bp. C.* (+667)

5.   The most cruel tortures inflicted on the martyrs were trifling, or as nothing in comparison with the martyrdom of Mary.

—*St. Anselm, O.S.B., Bp. C.*
Doctor of the Church (+1109)

6.   He suffered in the flesh, and she in the heart.

—*Blessed Amadeus, Cist.* (+1159)

7.   And why, O Lady, did you also go to sacrifice yourself on Calvary? Was not a crucified God sufficient to redeem us, that you, His Mother, would also go to be crucified with Him?

—*St. Bonaventure, O.F.M., Bp. C.*
Doctor of the Church (+1274)

8.   *Now there stood by the Cross of Jesus His Mother* (John 19:25).

Whereas other martyrs sacrifice their own lives, the Blessed Virgin consummated her martyrdom by sacrificing the life of her Son, a life which she loved far more than her own, and which exceeded all other torments ever endured by any mortal on earth.

—*St. Antoninus, O.P., Bp. C.* (+1459)

9.   Consider how love draws all the pains, all the torments, all the sufferings, all the sorrows, the wounds, the Passion, the Cross, and even the death of Our Redeemer into the Heart of His most Holy Mother. Alas, the same nails that crucify this Divine Child crucify also the Heart of the Mother; the same thorns which pierce His head, pierce the soul of that most gentle Mother. Through her condolence she had the same sorrows that her Son suffered; the same Passion through compassion, in a word, the sword of death which pierced the Body of this well-beloved Son, likewise pierced the Heart of that most loving Mother, inasmuch as the Heart of the Mother was one with her Son in so perfect a union that nothing could wound the one without also wounding the other. Her maternal breast thus wounded by love, far from seeking the cure of her wound, loved it more than any healing, cherishing the marks of sorrow that love has engraved on her Heart, and desiring continually to die of this wound since her Son had died of it amid the flames of charity, a perfect holocaust for all the sins of the world.

—*St. Francis de Sales, Bp. C.*
Doctor of the Church (+1622)

XXIII

Co-Redemptrix of the Human Race

1.   *Who finds me finds life, and draws salvation from the Lord.*
—(Prov. 8:35)

2.   The Eternal Son of God becomes Man by assuming our weak nature, but it is with Mary's consent that He does so.... Christ, for Whom the nations wait, comes at last, but He is born of Mary and, if the Shepherds and the Magi, first-fruits of the Faith, hasten piously to the Manger, it is with Mary they find the Child. When the Child wills to be brought to the Temple, in order to offer Himself by a public ceremony as a Victim to His Heavenly Father, it is still by the ministry of His Mother that He is presented to the Lord.... In the Garden of Gethsemane where Jesus is stricken with fear and is sad and sorrowful unto death; in the Pretorium where He is scourged, Mary is not indeed seen to be present, but she has long and distinctly known what sorrows are the destined portion of her Child. When she offered herself as a handmaid to become His Mother, and when she consecrated her entire self with Him in the Temple, she became from that moment by both of those actions, the associate of her Son in the toilsome work of expiation for the human race. Assuredly, she shares in her soul to an immense degree in the bitter anguish and distressing torment of her only Child. It was in her presence and under her eyes that the Divine Sacrifice was to be consummated and it was with this Sacrifice in view that the pure-souled magnanimous Virgin formed Him of her flesh, and fed Him with her milk.... Mary, His Mother, stood by the Cross of Jesus. She was on fire with a limitless love for us and, in order to have us for children, offered her own Child to the Divine Justice, died in spirit with Him the while her Heart was pierced with a sword of many sorrows.

—*Pope Leo XIII* (+1903)

3.   Her merciful office appears perhaps in no other form of prayer so manifestly as it does in the Rosary. For in the Rosary the part that Mary took as our co-Redemptress is set before us, as though the facts were even then taking place.

—*Pope Leo XIII* (+1903)

4.   By this participation in the sufferings and feelings of Jesus,

Mary merited to share in the Redemption of fallen humanity
and consequently to become the Almoner of all the treasures
that Jesus amassed for us by His bloody Death.

—*Pope St. Pius* X (+1914)

5.   She offered her Son so generously in sacrifice to satisfy the
justice of God that it may be said with reason that she cooper-
ated in the salvation of the human race along with Christ.

—*Pope Benedict* XV (+1922)

6.   As Eve, becoming disobedient, became the cause of death
both to herself and the whole human race, so also Mary, bearing
the predestined Man, and being yet a virgin, being obedient,
became both to herself and to the whole human race the cause
of salvation.

—*St. Irenaeus, Bp. M.* (+c. 202)

7.   O Blessed Virgin Mary, who can worthily repay you your
just dues of praise and thanksgiving, you who by the wondrous
assent of your will did rescue a fallen world? What songs of
praise can our weak human nature recite in your honor, since it
is by your intervention alone that it has found the way to
restoration?

—*St. Augustine, Bp. C.*
Doctor of the Church (+430)

8.   By you, O Mary, the Trinity is glorified; by you the precious Cross is celebrated and reverenced throughout the whole
world. By you mankind, which was enslaved by the errors of
idolatry, has been converted to the truth; believers have been
baptized; churches are everywhere erected. By your aid, nations
have done penance. What more can be said? By you the only-
begotten Son of God, that true Light, has shined on those that

were in darkness, and in the shadow of death. Who can worthily celebrate your praises, O Mother and Virgin!

—*St. Cyril of Alexandria, Bp. C.*
Doctor of the Church (+444)

9. O Virgin most holy, none abounds in the knowledge of God except through you; none, O Mother of God, attains salvation except through you; none receives a gift from the throne of mercy except through you.

—*St. Germanus of Constantinople, Bp. C.* (+c. 732)

10. Devotion to you, O Mary, is a pledge of salvation which God grants to those whom He wills to save.

—*St. John Damascene, Pr. C.*
Doctor of the Church (+c. 749)

11. O Blessed Mother of God, open to us the gate of Mercy: for you are the salvation of the human race.

—*St. John Damascene, Pr. C.*
Doctor of the Church (+c. 749)

12. God would not become Man without the consent of Mary: in the first place, that we might feel ourselves under great obligations to her, and secondly, that we might understand that the salvation of all is left to the care of this Blessed Virgin.

—*St. Peter Damian, Bp. C.*
Doctor of the Church (+1072)

13. Although God could create the world out of nothing, yet when it was lost by sin, He would not repair the evil without the cooperation of Mary.

—*St. Anselm, O.S.B., Bp. C.*
Doctor of the Church (+1109)

14. Through you, O Mother of love, O Mother of salvation, who has found grace with God, we find access to the Father, so that through you we are received by Him Who has been given to us through you. You are the dispenser of all graces; our salvation is in your hands.

—*St. Bernard of Clairvaux, Cist.*
Doctor of the Church (+1153)

15. God has deposited in Mary the fullness of all that is good, so that if we have any hope, any grace, any salvation, we should know that all comes to us by Mary.

—*St. Bernard of Clairvaux, Cist.*
Doctor of the Church (+1153)

16. See, O man, the designs of God—designs by which He is able to dispense His mercy more abundantly to us; for, desiring to redeem the whole human race, He has placed the whole price of Redemption in the hands of Mary, that she may dispense it at will.

—*St. Bernard of Clairvaux, Cist.*
Doctor of the Church (+1153)

17. All men, past, present and to come, should look upon Mary as the means and negotiator of the salvation of all ages.

—*St. Bernard of Clairvaux, Cist.*
Doctor of the Church (+1153)

18. When God was about to redeem the human race, He deposited the whole price in Mary's hands.

—*St. Bernard of Clairvaux, Cist.*
Doctor of the Church (+1153)

19. You have gone, O Virgin, in the salvation of your people: to their salvation with Christ. O blessed one, in your hands is laid up our salvation: be mindful O loving one, of our poverty. He

whom you will save, will be saved: and he from whom you shall turn away your face, will go down to destruction.

—*St. Bonaventure, O.F.M., Bp. C.*
Doctor of the Church (+1274)

20. By you redemption has been sent from God: the repentant people shall have the hope of salvation. . . . The way to come to Christ is to approach her: he who shall fly her shall not find the way of peace. . . . Approach to Our Lord to pray for us: that by you our sins may be blotted out. . . may sinners find grace with God by you, the finder of grace and salvation.

—*St. Bonaventure, O.F.M., Bp. C.*
Doctor of the Church (+1274)

21. It is a great thing in any saint to have grace sufficient for the salvation of many souls; but to have (as Mary had) enough to suffice for the salvation of everybody in the world, is the greatest of all.

—*St. Thomas Aquinas, O.P., C.*
Doctor of the Church (+1274)

22. Mary is after God and with God and under God the *efficient* cause of our regeneration because she begot our Redeemer, and because by her virtue, she merited by a merit of congruity this impeccable honor. She is the *material* cause, because the Holy Ghost through the intermediary of her consent took from her pure flesh and blood the flesh and blood from which was made the Body immolated for the Redemption of the world. She is the *final* cause, for the great work of Redemption which is ordained principally for the glory of God, is ordained second-arily for the honor of this same Virgin. She is the *formal* cause, for by the Light of a Light so very deiform she is the universal exemplar which shows us the way out of darkness to the vision of the Eternal Light.

—*St. Albertus Magnus, O.P., Pr. C.*
Doctor of the Church (+1280)

23. Our salvation is in her hands.

—*Blessed Raymond Jordano, Ab.* (+1381)

24. O Lady, since you are the dispenser of all graces, and since the grace of salvation can only come through your hands, our salvation depends on you.

—*St. Bernardine of Siena, O.F.M.* (+1444)

25. *I will put enmities between you and the woman, and your seed and her seed: she shall crush your head* (Gen. 3:15). Who could this woman, the serpent's victor, be but Mary, who by her fair humility and holy life always conquered him and beat down his strength? The Mother of Our Lord Jesus Christ was promised in the person of that woman, as it is remarked by St. Cyprian (*De Viro perf. inter op. S. Hier.*), and after him another ancient writer; and therefore God did not say "I put," but "I *will* put," lest He might seem to refer to Eve,...to signify that the serpent's opponent was not to be Eve, who was then living, but would be another woman descending from her, and who, as St. Vincent Ferrer observes, "would bring our first parents far greater advantages than those which they had lost by their sin" (*Serm. de Concep. B.V.M.*).... St. Bruno says that "Eve was the cause of death," by allowing herself to be overcome by the serpent, "But that Mary," by conquering the devil, "restored life to us" (*De B.V., s.* 2).

—*St. Alphonsus Liguori, C.SS.R., Bp. C.*
Doctor of the Church (+1787)

XXIV

Mother of the Mystical Body

1.   O Virgin most pure, whose privilege it is to approach your Son without fear of rebuff! Beseech Him, O Virgin most holy,

to grant peace to the world and to breathe into the Churches of Christendom one mind and one heart; and we shall all magnify you.

—*Breviary of the Greek Church, 5 May*
Office of St. Irene, V.M., Theotokion after hymn IX

2. *Behold your son.* Now in John—such has been the constant tradition of the Church—Christ designated the whole human race, and in the first rank are they who are joined with Him by faith.... With a generous heart Mary undertook and discharged the duties of her high but laborious office, the beginnings of which were concentrated in the Cenacle. With wonderful care she nurtured the first Christians by her holy example, her authoritative counsel, her sweet consolation, her fruitful prayers. She was, in very truth, the Mother of the Church, the teacher and Queen of the Apostles, to whom, besides, she confided no small part of the divine oracles which she kept in her heart.

—*Pope Leo XIII* (+1903)

3. The Mother of our Head, in bearing Him corporally became spiritually the Mother of all the members of this Divine Head—*Corpore mater capitis nostri, spiritu mater membrorum ejus.*

—*St. Augustine, Bp. C.*
Doctor of the Church (+430)

4. Mother of God! be mindful of Christians who are your servants; commend the prayers of all; help all to realize their hopes; strengthen the Faith; keep the Church in unity.

—*St. Germanus of Constantinople, Bp. C.*(+c. 732)

5. What dignity, O Virgin, could be more highly prized than to be the Mother of those of whom Christ deigned to be Father and Brother?

—*St. Anselm, O.S.B., Bp. C.*
Doctor of the Church (+1109)

6. Since Mary has formed Jesus Christ, the Head of the elect, it is also her office to form the members of that Head, that is to say, all true Christians; for a mother does not form the head without the members, nor the members without the head. Whoever, therefore, wishes to be a member of Jesus Christ, full of grace and truth, must be formed in Mary by means of the grace of Jesus Christ, which she possesses in its fullness, in order to communicate it fully to her children, the true members of Jesus Christ.

—*St. Louis-Marie Grignon de Montfort* (+1716)

XXV

Mother of Priests

1. The Heart of the Glorious Virgin contributed to the work of our Redemption, because Jesus Christ, Who is both the Victim Who was sacrificed for our salvation and the Priest Who immolated the Victim, is the fruit of her Heart.

—*St. John Eudes, Pr. C.* (+1680)

XXVI

Queen of Apostles

1. Rejoice, for you alone have destroyed the heresies of the entire world.

—*An Office of Our Lady*

2. Hail, O Mouth ever eloquent of the Apostles, O firm foundation of the Faith, O unassailable rampart of the Church!

—*From the Akathistos hymn*

3.   It is no exaggeration to say that it is chiefly under Mary's patronage and by her aid that the doctrine and laws of the Gospel have spread so rapidly in spite of immense obstacles and difficulties, amongst all nations and across continents, inaugurating everywhere a new order of justice and peace....Moreover, as St. Cyril of Alexandria has declared, it is she who has planted and consolidated the sceptre of the True Faith; she has always unceasingly worked to maintain firm, wholesome and fruitful the Catholic Faith. There are many well-known facts to prove this. Some of them even forced themselves on the attention of men by the wonderful circumstances surrounding them. It is above all at times and in places where faith has grown lamentably languid through indifference, or has been weakened by the pernicious scourge of heresy and error that the pitying aid of the August Virgin has made itself felt. At such times men eminent in holiness and apostolic zeal, guided by her suggestions, and relying on her assistance, have arisen to thrust back the onslaughts of the wicked and to lead souls to the holiness of Christian life. She is the Seat of Divine Wisdom, and the Fathers and Doctors of the Church gratefully attribute to her inspiration the writings with which they have enriched the Church, and in consequence they proclaim that by her and not by themselves has the malice of error been confounded.

—*Pope Leo XIII* (+1903)

4.   Hail Mary, for by you the Son of God gives light to them that sit in darkness and the shadow of death; by you the prophets have spoken; by you, the Apostles preached salvation to the nations; by you the Holy Cross is hallowed and venerated in all the world; by you the wicked angels have been routed, and Heaven restored to fallen man, by you souls chained in the errors of idolatry come back to the way of knowledge and of the truth; by you the faithful come to holy Baptism and churches have been established among all peoples of the earth.

—*St. Cyril of Alexandria, Bp. C.*
Doctor of the Church (+444)

5.   Hail, Marvelous fountain whence gushed forth the waters of Divine Wisdom, the clear and limpid waters of orthodoxy that rolled back the flood of error.

> —*St. Germanus of Constantinople, Bp. C.* (+c. 732)

6.   Hail, O you by whom we have been numbered among the citizens of the One, Holy, Catholic, Apostolic Church!

> —*St. John Damascene, Pr. C.*
> *Doctor of the Church* (+c. 749)

XXVII

Mother of Us All

1.   *I will bless you, and I will multiply your seed as the stars of Heaven, and as the sand that is by the seashore.*

> —(Gen. 20:17)

2.   The mystery of Christ's wondrous love towards us shines out more especially in the fact that when dying He bequeathed His Mother to John the disciple as his mother, in His thoughtful testament: *Behold your son.* But, as the Church has always felt, in John Christ would signify the person of the human race, more especially those who would cling to Him by faith. Thus St. Anselm of Canterbury: "What more fitting, then, that you, O Virgin, should be the Mother of those whose Father and Brother Christ designed to be?" (*Oratio xlvii*). She, then, undertook her share in this exclusive and toilsome task and died great of soul amidst the consecrated token in the Upper Room.

> —*Pope Leo XIII* (+1903)

3.   From the very fact that the most Holy Virgin is the Mother of Jesus Christ she is the Mother of all Christians, whom she

bore on Mount Calvary amid the supreme throes of the Redemption; Jesus Christ is, in a manner, the Firstborn of Christians, we by adoption and Redemption are His brothers.

—*Pope Leo XIII* (+1903)

4.   For is not Mary the Mother of God? Then she is our Mother also. And we must in truth hold that Christ, the Word made flesh, is also the Savior of mankind. He had a physical body like that of any other man; and again, as Savior of the human family, He had a spiritual and Mystical Body, the society, namely, of those who believe in Christ: *We, being many, are one Body in Christ* (Rom. 12:5). Now, the Blessed Virgin did not conceive the Eternal Son of God merely in order that He might be made Man, taking His human nature from her, but also in order that by means of the nature He assumed from her He might be the Redeemer of men. For which reason the Angel said to the shepherds: *Today there is born to you a Savior, Who is Christ the Lord* (Luke 2:2). Wherefore, in the same holy bosom of His most chaste Mother, Christ took to Himself flesh, and united to Himself the spiritual body formed by those who were to believe in Him. Hence Mary, carrying the Savior within her, may be said to have also carried all those whose life was contained in the life of the Savior. Therefore, all we who are united to Christ and, as the Apostle says, are *members of His Body, of His flesh, and of His bones* (Eph. 5:30), have issued from the womb of Mary and she is the *Mother of us all.* "Mother, spiritually indeed, but truly Mother of the members of Christ, which we are" (St. Augustine: *De sancta Virginitate,* cap. 6). If, then, the Blessed Virgin is the Mother at once of God and men, who can doubt that she will work with all diligence to procure that Christ, *the Head of the Body the Church* (Col. 1:18), may transfuse His gifts unto us, His members, and, above all, that of knowing Him and living through Him (1 John 4:9)?

—*Pope St. Pius X* (+1914)

5.   It is clear, too, that this most sorrowful Virgin, since

appointed by Jesus Christ, as the Mother of all men, received them as a testament of infinite charity left to her, and fulfills with motherly kindness the task of forwarding their spiritual life; nor can she fail more especially to assist these most dear adopted children in that hour when it is a question of confirming unto eternity their salvation and sanctity.

—*Pope Benedict XV* (+1922)

6.   May Mary, the most holy Queen of Apostles, kindly smile on all and prosper the work undertaken; for since on Calvary all men were entrusted to her motherly care, she does not less cherish and love those who are ignorant of the fact that they are redeemed by Jesus Christ, than she does those who happily enjoy the benefits of that Redemption.

—*Pope Pius XI* (+1939)

7.   When the little Maid of Nazareth uttered her *fiat* to the message of the angel and the Word was made flesh in her womb, she became not only the Mother of God in the physical order of nature but also in the supernatural order of grace she became the Mother of all, who through the Holy Spirit would be made one under the headship of her Divine Son. The Mother of the Head would be the Mother of the members. The Mother of the Vine would be the Mother of the branches.

—*Pope Pius XII* (+1958)

8.   *Venter tuus sicut acervus tritici, vallatus liliis* (Cant. 7:2). Although in the most pure womb of Mary there was but one grain of corn, which was Jesus Christ, yet it is called a heap of wheat, because all the elect were virtually contained in it; and as she was also to be their Mother, in bringing forth Jesus He was truly called the first-born of many brethren.

—*St. Ambrose, Bp. C.*
Doctor of the Church (+397)

9.   True it is, according to the exterior the whole race of man upon earth was born from Eve; but in reality it is from Mary that Life is truly born to the world, so that by giving birth to the Living One, Mary might also become the Mother of all the living.

—*St. Epiphanius, Ab., Bp. C.* (+403)

10. Through you do the miserable obtain mercy, the ungracious grace, sinners pardon, the weak strength, the worldly heavenly things, mortals life, and pilgrims their country.

—*St. Augustine, Bp. C.*
Doctor of the Church (+430)

11. At the same moment when Mary consented to become the Mother of God, she also consented to become the Mother of all the children of salvation, and bore them already at that time beneath her Heart.

—*St. Bernardine of Siena, O.F.M.* (+1444)

12. It is true that according to the prophecy of Isaias, Jesus, in dying for the Redemption of the human race, chose to be alone. *I have trodden the winepress alone* (Is. 63:3); but, seeing the ardent desire of Mary to aid in the salvation of man, He disposed it so that she, by the sacrifice and offering of the life of her Jesus, should cooperate in our salvation, and thus become the Mother of our souls. This Our Savior signified when, before expiration, He looked down from the Cross on His Mother and on the disciple St. John, who stood at its foot, and, first addressing Mary, He said, *Behold your son,* as it were saying, Behold the whole human race, which by the offer you make of My life for the salvation of all, is even now being born to the life of grace. Then turning to the disciple, He said, *Behold your Mother.* "By these words," says St. Bernardine of Siena, "Mary, by reason of the love she bore them, became the Mother, not only of St. John, but of all men." And Silveira (Goncalo da Silveira, S.J.,

martyred 1651) remarks that St. John himself, in stating this fact in his Gospel, says: "Then he said to the disciple, *Behold your Mother*. Here observe well that Jesus did not address Himself to John but to 'the disciple,' in order to show that He then gave Mary to all who are His disciples, that is to say, to all Christians, that she might be their Mother." Further says Silveira, "John is but the name of one, whereas the word disciple is applicable to all; therefore Our Lord makes use of a name common to all, to show that Mary was given to us."

> —*St. Alphonsus Liguori, C.SS.R., Bp. C.*
> *Doctor of the Church* (+1787)

13. My daughters! Rejoice and be glad to have the Blessed Virgin for your Mother. Serve her with great joy, for she well deserves it. Go to her in all your straits and you will always come out successfully.

> —*St. Joachima Vedruna de Mas* (+1854)

14. O Mary, I have no longer a mother on earth! From henceforth be you my mother!

> —*St. Gemma, C.P., V.* (+1903)

15. Every May I think at all times on the great benefits I have received from my heavenly Mother, even from my tenderest years.

> —*St. Gemma, C.P., V.* (+1903)

16. Grant me, O Mary, that I may get to know the cross; not only Jesus' Cross, but whatever cross fits me best.

> —*St. Gemma, C.P., V.* (+1903)

17. Jesus entrusted me to his Mother, and charged me to love her very much. You are then my heavenly Mother. You will be towards me like any mother towards her children. You see me weak? You will have mercy on my weakness. You see me poor

in virtue? You will help me. O my mother, do not forsake me! My dearest Mother, do not abandon me!

—*St. Gemma, C.P., V.* (+1903)

18. O Mary, I want to be always your child.

—*St. Dominic Savio* (+1857)

19. We are all children of Eve according to the flesh, and of the Virgin according to the spirit. She has for all the love of a mother and the courage of a defender. See how great she must be to be the Mother of so many children. Just as well as sinners, all find room in her: sinners find pardon through her prayers, and the just are preserved in grace. If He Who is larger than heaven and earth, could find room in her, do you think you sinner will not be able to find room in her? Mary is roomier than the earth. Just and sinners alike find entrance into her. God entered into her and abides in her.

—*St. John of Avila* (+1569)

XXVIII

Her Falling Asleep and Assumption

1. Receive, O Lord, the gifts we offer You on this once more recurring solemnity of Blessed Mary, because to Your praise and glory it redounds, that even thus she was assumed.

—*An Offertory of the Mass for 15 August*

2. The ineffable mystery of this solemn day of the Mother of God is the more to be exalted, because the day is an exceptional one, owing to the Assumption of the Virgin, whose virginal integrity won for her her Son, and whose death was without parallel.... By her Assumption she felt not the corruption of

death, she who bore the Author of life. With earnest prayers let us entreat the Lord, dear brethren, that through His mercy we may at our death escape hell and (our souls) be born also where *the* body of the Blessed Virgin was transported from the tomb.

—From the Gothic Missal, c. Sixth Century
Used in Spain before the Mozarabic, and later in France

3.   May today's venerable festivity, O Lord, bring us salutary aid, whereon God's Holy Mother underwent temporal death, yet, *could not be held down by the shackles of death*, she who bore Your Son made flesh of her.

—Gregorian Sacramentary, Sixth Century

4.   The queenly figure of Mary is illuminated and glorified in the highest dignity which a creature may attain. What grace, sweetness and solemnity in the scene of Mary's "falling asleep," as the Christians of the East imagine it! She is lying in the serene sleep of death; Jesus stands beside her, and clasps her soul as if it were a tiny child, to his heart, to indicate the miracle of her immediate resurrection and glorification.

The Christians of the West, raising their eyes and hearts to heaven, choose to portray Mary borne body and soul to the eternal kingdom. The greatest artists saw her thus, incomparable in her divine beauty. Oh let us go with her, borne aloft by her escort of angels!

This is the source of consolation and faith, in days of grief or pain, for those privileged souls—such as we all can become, if only we respond to grace—whom God is silently preparing for the most beautiful victory of all, the attainment of holiness.

The great mission which began with the angel's announcement to Mary has passed like a stream of fire and light through the mysteries in turn: God's eternal plan for our salvation has been presented to us in one scene after another, accompanying us along our way, and now it brings us back to God in the splendor of heaven.

The glory of Mary, Mother of Jesus and our mother too, is

irradiated in the inaccessible light of the august Trinity and reflected in the dazzling splendor in Holy Church, triumphant in heaven, suffering patiently in purgatory in the confident expectation of heaven, and militant on earth.

—*Pope John XXIII* (+1963)

5.   Eve was the cause of death for men, because through her death came into the world. But Mary was the cause of life, for through her Life was born unto us.

—*St. Epiphanius, Ab., Bp. C.* (+403)

6.   Mary's holy body is enjoying the bliss worthy of her through whom light shone upon the world. . . . In her immortal and glorified body, she received the reward of her chastity and of her martyrdom: These things are certain beyond doubt for me.

—*St. Epiphanius, Ab., Bp. C.* (+403)

7.   One day, the Feast of the Assumption of Our Lady, Queen of Angels, the Lord desired to grant me the following favor; in a rapture he showed me her ascent to heaven, the happiness and solemnity with which she was received, and the place where she is. The glory my spirit experienced in seeing so much glory was magnificent. The effects of this favor were great. . . I was left with a longing to serve Our Lady since she deserved this so much.

—*St. Teresa of Avila*
Doctor of the Church (+1582)

8.   Today the blessed Apostles and holy virgins gathered together and arrayed in glittering white garments, lit their lamps and sang: "Blessed are you, yes, thrice blessed among women."

Today while the most Holy Virgin reposed in the sepulchre, they waited and hoped for the coming of the Lord, and they beheld the Creator come from on high amid the Angels, and in accord with them they said: "Blessed are you, yes, thrice blessed among women."

Today they have beheld the most Holy Virgin borne aloft and ascending to Heaven upon a chariot of clouds, to enter there with the prudent virgins, and sing: "Blessed are you, yes, thrice blessed among women." . . .

Today the Angels bore *the most pure body of the Mother of God* from the lower to the higher sphere; therefore it is that the Church with jubilee chants her new hymns.

—*Ancient Armenian Breviary*

9.   Mary conceived without detriment to her virginity, gave birth to her Son without pain, and *departed hence without being subject to corruption*, conformably to the word of the Angel, or rather of God speaking by the Angel, in order that she might be shown to be full, not half full, of grace; and that God, her Son, might faithfully observe the ancient commandment which He had long since given, that is to say, to forestall with honor one's father and mother; and lest the virginal flesh of Christ, which had been taken from the flesh of the Virgin Mother, should be at variance with the whole.

—*Pope Alexander III (+1181)*

10. If the Church, besides celebrating on 15 August and the following days the Assumption of the Blessed Virgin into Heaven, proposes to the Faithful the homilies of St. John Damascene and St. Bernard, which in the clearest terms assert that she was taken up to Heaven in body as well as in soul, there can be no doubt, it seems, on which side lies the weight of Her authority and Her verdict.

—*Pope Benedict XIV (+1758)*

11. *The Queen stood on the right hand in gilded clothing, surrounded with variety* (Ps. 44:10). We read how the angels have come to the death and burial of some of the saints, and how they have accompanied the souls of the elect to Heaven with hymns and

praises. How much more should we believe that the heavenly army, with all its bands, came forth rejoicing in festal array, to meet the Mother of God, surrounded her with effulgent light, and led her with praises and canticles to the throne prepared for her from the beginning of the world.

—*St. Jerome, Pr. C.*
Doctor of the Church (+420)

12. This venerable day has dawned, the day that surpasses all the festivals of the saints, this most exalted and most solemn day on which the Blessed Virgin was assumed body and soul into heavenly glory. On this day the queenly Virgin was exalted to the very throne of God the Father, and elevated to such a height that the angelic spirits are in admiration.

—*St. Augustine, Bp. C.*
Doctor of the Church (+430)

13. I hold that Mary is in Christ and with Christ: in Christ, because in Him we live and move and have our being; with Christ, because she is assumed into glory.

—*St. Augustine, Bp. C.*
Doctor of the Church (+430)

14. The Lord had the most holy body (of the Virgin) taken into Heaven, where reunited to her soul, it now enjoys with the elect happiness without end.... Mary, the glorious Mother of Christ, was taken up into Heaven by the Lord, while the angelic choirs sang hymns of joy.

—*St. Gregory of Tours, Bp. C.* (+593)

15. God Himself from on high sent a legion of angels to transport to Him His holy Ark—that Ark whereof David, Mary's ancestor, had sung: *Arise, O Lord, into your resting-place: You and the Ark which You have sanctified....* Incomparable Ark, not made by the hand of man, but by that of God; not covered with

material gold, but all resplendent with the flames of the holy and life-giving Spirit Who came down upon her. Christ, the Son of God, Whom Mary ever-Virgin, through the operation of the Holy Ghost, had clothed with flesh, quickened by a rational soul, had called her to Himself, and has in turn clothed her with incorruptibility like His own, and crowning her with the unrivaled glory, has bidden her enter upon a share of His inheritance: for she is His own most Holy Mother. Thus is fulfilled the word of the Psalmist: The Queen stood on Your right hand, in gilded clothing surrounded with variety.... O happy Repose of the glorious, ever-Virgin Mary, whose body, wherein Life was enclosed, did not suffer the corruption of the grave, being safeguarded by the omnipotence of Christ our Savior, Who was formed from that virginal flesh.... Hail, most Holy Mother of God! Jesus, Son of God and King of glory, Who had chosen you to be His spiritual palace here on earth, that, at the same time, He might through you bestow on us His heavenly Kingdom, has willed to have you with Him in that Kingdom, *intact of body* and glorious above all, to the glory of His Father and the Holy Spirit.

—St. Modestus (+634)

16. Let no one refuse to believe so surprising a miracle. Remember Elias and Enoch, both caught up to Heaven, without passing through the dust of the tomb.... A woman, whose purity surpasses that of the heavens, penetrating the depths of Heaven, with the tabernacle of her body; a Virgin, whom a miraculous childbirth had exalted far above the Seraphim, rising aloft nigh unto God, the Author of all being; the Mother of Life exhibiting to us in her person an ending like that of her blessed Fruit, a miracle worthy of God and of our faith.

—St. Andrew of Crete (+720)

17. He has done two astounding things, one in His own life-giving sepulchre, the other in yours, which He has quickened with life. For both have in truth received your bodies, but

neither has delivered them to decay. Again, it was impossible that this vessel of your body, which was filled with God, should crumble away into dust like our common flesh. Since He Who annihilated Himself within you is God from the beginning, and hence Life before all ages, the Mother of Life must dwell together with Life; she must lie in death, as in a momentary slumber, and the passing of this Mother of Life must be as an awakening from sleep.

—*St. Germanus of Constantinople, Bp. C.* (+c. 732)

18. True, you were laid in the tomb even as we, but that tomb left empty is a proof that you have been drawn up from this perishable life to the immortal life of Heaven.

—*St. Germanus of Constantinople, Bp. C.* (+c. 732)

19. It has been handed down to us from of old, that at the time of the glorious Passing of Our Lady, all the holy Apostles who were then toiling in various parts of the world for the salvation of mankind were in an instant caught up into the air, and borne together to Jerusalem. There a vision of angels appeared to them, and they heard the chant of Angelic Powers. And thus with glory to God, she yielded up her blessed soul into the hands of her Maker. As for her body, which in an ineffable manner had harbored God, it was carried out for burial amid the hymns of Angels and of the Apostles, and was laid in a tomb at Gethsemani, and for three days the songs of Angels continued without ceasing. At the end of the three days the melody of the Angels ceased, and Thomas, who alone had been absent, having come on the third day, and desiring to pay homage to that body which had harbored God, the Apostles opened the tomb, but search as they would, nowhere could they discover the sacred body. They found only the clothes in which it had been enshrouded and being refreshed with the ineffable fragrance which proceeded from them, they once more closed the tomb. Astounded at the extraordinary and mysterious event, they could but conclude, that He Whom it had pleased to take

flesh of the Virgin Mary, and of her to be made Man and to be born—though He was God the Word and the Lord of glory—and Who had kept her virginity unimpaired even after child-birth, had also been pleased, upon her departure hence, to shield her sinless body from decay, and to honor it by removal hence before the common and universal resurrection. There were present then together with the Apostles the most holy Timothy, the first Bishop of the Ephesians, and Dionysius the Areopagite, as he himself attests in what he wrote to the afore-said Timothy with reference to Blessed Hieromtheus, who was also present on that occasion. ("Once he has spoken, any further speech is out of place:" so the Areopagite). "For even among our Divinely inspired Pontiffs he shone, as you yourself were witness, when, as you remember, we also and many of our holy brethren had come together to view that body which had given birth to Life, and harbored God. There were present James, the brother of the Lord, and Peter, supreme head and eldest of theologians, and having seen the sacred body, we were all pleased to chant, as each one might, the praises of the infinite goodness and power of God."

—St. John Damascene, Pr. C.
Doctor of the Church (+c. 749)

20. Your stainless body did not remain within the earth; you were transported alive to the royal abode of Heaven—you who are at once Queen, Mistress and Sovereign, and very truly the Mother of God.... How could she taste death who has given Life to all? She does, indeed, submit to the law enacted by Him Whom she bore; and as a daughter of the old Adam, she sub-mits to the sentence passed of old—for her Son, though He is Life itself, did not exempt Himself from it. But as the Mother of the living God, she is worthily taken up to Him.

—St. John Damascene, Pr. C.
Doctor of the Church (+c. 749)

21. She has left us in body, but her spirit is with us; from

Heaven she puts to flight the demons, having become our Mediatrix with God. Death, introduced into the world by Eve, oppressed the earth with a cruel tyranny. Today, seeking to assail the blessed daughter of a guilty mother, death was put to flight, and its downfall has come from the same source from which it had formerly its power. Holy Virgin, *I behold you asleep, rather than dead*; you are borne from earth to Heaven and from there you cease not to protect the human race. O Mother, you were ever a Virgin, because God was your blessed Fruit. And that is why your death is life, not as our death: for you are incorrupt in body and in soul.

—*St. Theodore Studites* (+826)

22. Our Savior ascends to Heaven by the power of His sovereign might, as Lord and Creator, accompanied by angels who pay Him homage, not dependent on their help or assistance. Mary is *assumed* into Heaven in virtue of an uplifting grace, escorted and upheld by the angels, raised aloft by grace, not by nature.... The whole multitude of the angels are gathered together, to see their Queen at the right of the Lord of hosts, in gilded vesture, in her ever immaculate body.

—*St. Peter Damian, Bp. C.*
Doctor of the Church (+1072)

23. O Glorious Virgin, who did submit to death, but could not be held in durance by the bonds of death: because you alone, O Virgin, did bear Him Who was the death of death, and of the grave the sting!

—*St. Anselm, O.S.B., Bp. C.*
Doctor of the Church (+1109)

24. It was precisely for this purpose that the Redeemer was pleased to ascend to Heaven before His Mother: He did so not only to prepare a throne for her in that Kingdom, but also that He might Himself accompany her with all the blessed spirits,

and thus render her entry into Heaven more glorious, and such
as became one who was His Mother.

—*St. Anselm, O.S.B., Bp. C.*
Doctor of the Church (+1109)

25. If the mind of man can never comprehend the immense
glory prepared in Heaven by God for those who on earth have
loved Him, as the Apostle tells us (1 Cor. 2:9), who can ever
comprehend the glory that He has prepared for His beloved
Mother who, more than all men, loved Him on earth; no, even
from the first moment of her creation, loved Him more than all
men and angels united?

—*St. Bernard of Clairvaux, Cist.*
Doctor of the Church (+1153)

26. Today she is welcomed by Him whom she herself welcomed
when He came to the hamlet of this earth of ours. But with what
honor, think you, He welcomed her, with what exaltation and
what glory! There was not on earth a worthier spot than the
temple of her virginal bosom, nor was there in Heaven a place
more exalted than the seat where Mary was enthroned by her
Divine Son. Happy twofold welcome! Hence we read today of
that woman who received Christ into her home (Gospel for
15 August, Luke 10:38-42), a reception that was an image of
Mary's reception into Heaven.... Who can conceive how
great was the glory of the Queen of the world, as she advanced,
or with what depth of devotion and affection the whole multitude of the heavenly legions went forth to meet her; with what
glad canticles she was conducted to her glorious throne; with
what placid mien, what serenity of countenance, what divine
embraces she was welcomed by her Son, and exalted above all
creatures, with the honor which such a Mother merited, and the
glory which became so great a Son?

—*St. Bernard of Clairvaux, Cist.*
Doctor of the Church (+1153)

27. *I will glorify the place of My feet* (Is. 60:13). Mary is the place to which the allusion is made. For the Lord's feet are His lowly human nature, and Mary is the sanctuary that harbored it. And today He has glorified this spot, raising it above the angels. Hence we have evidently her glorious Assumption. That is why it was said: *Arise, O Lord into Your resting-place: You and the Ark which You have sanctified.* (Ps. 131:8). The Lord arose when He ascended to the right hand of the Father. The ark which He has sanctified arose when the Virgin Mother was assumed to the heavenly bridal chamber. Go forth and contemplate admiringly the Mother of the King in the diadem wherewith her Son crowned her in the day of her triumph and glorious Assumption.

> —*St. Anthony of Padua, O.F.M.*
> *Doctor of the Church* (+1231)

28. The last curse common to man and woman lies in this, that they must return to dust; and from this Mary was free. We believe that after her death she was restored to life and carried to Heaven, according to verse 8, Psalm 121, a text very often applied by early Christian writers to the twofold resurrection of Our Lord and His Blessed Mother, she being the true Ark of the Covenant, which the Lord has sanctified.

> —*St. Thomas Aquinas, O.P., C.*
> *Doctor of the Church* (+1274)

29. The flower perishes in death, as it is said in Isaias: *The grass is withered, and the flower is fallen.* It will flower again in a glorious resurrection, according to the Psalmist: *My flesh has flowered again.* This flower of the glorification of the body has, as it were, as many petals as the glorified body has gifts and rewards. And certainly the holy Doctors seem to hold it as probable, and strive with some show of reason to prove, that the Blessed Virgin was taken up body and soul into Heaven, and that her body and soul are now in glory.

> —*St. Bonaventure, O.F.M., Bp. C.*
> *Doctor of the Church* (+1274)

30. When the glorious Virgin was assumed into Heaven, she augmented the joy of all its inhabitants.

> —*St. Bonaventure, O.F.M., Bp. C.*
> *Doctor of the Church* (+1274)

31. (After citing many evidences, Scriptural and Patristic, he concludes:) For these reasons and from these arguments based on authority, as well as many others, it is plain that the most Blessed Mother of God has been assumed in body and soul beyond the choirs of angels. And this in every way we believe to be true.

> —*St. Albertus Magnus, O.P., Pr. C.*
> *Doctor of the Church* (+1280)

32. Jesus, to honor the triumph of His most sweet Mother, went forth in His glory to meet and accompany her.

> —*St. Bernardine of Siena, O.F.M.* (+1444)

33. If this Mother lived her Son's life, she also died her Son's death. . . . Having collected in her spirit all the most beloved mysteries of the life and death of her Son by a most lively and continued memory of them, and withal, ever receiving directly the most ardent inspirations which her Child, the Sun of Justice

has cast upon human beings, in the highest noon of His charity; and besides, making on her part also, a perpetual movement of contemplation, at length the sacred fire of this divine love consumed her entirely as a holocaust of sweetness, so that she died thereof, the soul being wholly ravished and transported into the arms of the dilection of her Son.

> —*St. Francis de Sales, Bp. C.*
> *Doctor of the Church* (+1622)

34. Cedrenus (Georgius Cedrenus, *Comp. Histor.*, n. 86), Nicephorus (Nicephorus Gregoras, *Hist.*, I. 2, c. 21) and Metaphrastes (Symeon Metaphrastes, *Or. de Vita et Dorm. M.* —for this writer see *Catholic Encyclopedia*, x, 225) relate that,

some days before her death, Our Lord sent her the Archangel
Gabriel, the same that announced to her that she was that
blessed woman chosen to be the Mother of God.... Many
authors, such as St. Andrew of Crete (*In Dorm. S. M.*, or. i), St.
John Damascene (*Hist.* I. 3, c. 40), Euthymius (*De Dorm B. M.*,
or. 1 et 2), assert that, before her death, the Apostles, and also
many disciples...assembled in Mary's room.

> —*St. Alphonsus Liguori, C.SS.R., Bp. C.*
> *Doctor of the Church* (+1787)

35. There are three things that render death bitter: attachment
to the world, remorse for sins, and the uncertainty of salvation.
The death of Mary was entirely free from these causes of bit-
terness, and was accompanied by three special graces, which
rendered it precious and full of joy. She died as she had lived,
entirely detached from the things of the world; she died in the
most perfect peace; she died in the certainty of eternal glory.

> —*St. Alphonsus Liguori, C.SS.R., Bp. C.*
> *Doctor of the Church* (+1787)

36. As the loving Virgin lived, so did she die. As Divine Love
gave her life, so did It cause her death; for the Doctors and holy
Fathers of the Church generally say she died of no other infir-
mity than pure love; St. Ildephonsus (+667) says that Mary
ought not to die, or only die of love.

> —*St. Alphonsus Liguori, C. SS. R., Bp. C.*
> *Doctor of the Church* (+1787)

XXIX

Sovereignty of Mary

1.   If the Son is a King, the Mother who begot Him is rightly

and truly considered a Queen and Sovereign.

—*St. Athanasius, Bp. C.*
Doctor of the Church (+373)

2.   *And He was subject to them* (Luke 2:51). Jesus Christ having deigned to make Mary His Mother, inasmuch as He was her Son He was truly obliged to obey her.

—*St. Ambrose, Bp. C.*
Doctor of the Church (+397)

3.   We truly confess her to be Queen of Heaven, because she brought forth the King of Angels.

—*St. Augustine, Bp. C.*
Doctor of the Church (+430)

4.   The greatest glory of the blessed in Heaven is, after seeing God, the presence of this most beautiful Queen.

—*St. Peter Damian, Bp. C.*
Doctor of the Church (+1072)

5.   Her Son esteems her prayers so greatly, and is so desirous to satisfy her, that when she prays it seems as if she rather commanded than prayed, and was rather a queen than a handmaid.

—*St. Peter Damian, Bp. C.*
Doctor of the Church (+1072)

6.   You, O Lady, are more exalted than the patriarchs, greater than the martyrs, more glorious than the confessors, purer than the virgins, and, therefore, you alone and without them, can accomplish what they can do only jointly with you.

—*St. Anselm, O.S.B., Bp. C.*
Doctor of the Church (+1109)

7.   *And a great sign appeared in heaven, a Woman clothed with the*

sun, and the moon under her feet, and on her head a crown of twelve stars (Apoc. 12:1). You O Lady, have clothed the Sun, that is the Eternal Word, with human flesh; but He has clothed you with His power and mercy.

—*St. Bernard of Clairvaux, Cist.*
Doctor of the Church (+1153)

8.   Why does the Church call Mary "the Queen of Mercy"? It is because we believe that she opens the abyss of the mercy of God to whomsoever she wills, when she wills, and as she wills; so that there is no sinner, however great, who is lost if Mary protects him.

—*St. Bernard of Clairvaux, Cist.*
Doctor of the Church (+1153)

9.   When the Blessed Virgin conceived the Eternal Word in her womb, and brought Him forth, she obtained half the Kingdom of God: so that she is Queen of Mercy as Jesus Christ is King of Justice.

—*St. Thomas Aquinas, O.P., C.*
Doctor of the Church (+1274)

10. Nay, more, whenever the most sacred Virgin goes to God to intercede for us, she, as Queen, commands all the angels and saints to accompany her, and unite their prayers to hers.

—*St. Bonaventure, O.F.M., Bp. C.* (+1274)

11. *Her throne is as the sun in My sight, and as the moon perfect for ever* (Ps. 88:38). The Lord has prepared for Mary eternal light in Heaven, so that, as the sinful soul, the throne of the devil, will be miraculously dark for ever, Mary, the Mediatrix, the throne of Christ, will be marvelously luminous for ever.

—*St. Bonaventure, O.F.M., Bp. C.*
Doctor of the Church (+1274)

12. At the command of Mary, all obey, even God.
                    —*St. Bernardine of Siena, O.F.M.* (+1444)

13. No sooner had Mary consented to be the Mother of the Eternal Word, than she merited by this consent to be made Queen of the world and of all creatures.
                    —*St. Bernardine of Siena, O.F.M.* (+1444)

14. God has placed the whole Church, not only under her patronage, but even under the dominion of Mary.
                    —*St. Antoninus, O.P., Bp. C.* (+1459)

15. The prayers of the Blessed Virgin, being the prayers of His Mother, have in them something of a command.
                    —*St. Antoninus, O.P., Bp. C.* (+1459)

16. Mary, then, is a Queen: but for our common consolation, be it known that she is a Queen so sweet, clement, and so ready to help us in our miseries, that Holy Church wills that we should salute her in this prayer (Salve Regina) under the title of Queen of Mercy.
                    —*St. Alphonsus Liguori, C.SS.R., Bp. C.*
                    Doctor of the Church (+1787)

17. Jesus, Who is omnipotent, made Mary also omnipotent; though of course it is always true that where the Son is omnipotent by nature, the Mother is so only by grace. But that she is so is evident from the fact that, whatever the Mother asks for, the Son never denies her.... This we know from what occurred at the marriage feast of Cana in Galilee. When the wine failed, the most Blessed Virgin, being moved to compassion at the sight of the affliction and shame of the bride and bridegroom, asked her Son to relieve them by a miracle, telling Him that *they had no wine.* Jesus answered, *Woman, what is that to you and Me? My hour is not yet come* (John 2:4).... Mary, who well knew her privilege, although her Son seemed to have refused

her the favor, yet told them to fill the jars with water, as if her request had already been granted. And so it was; for Jesus, to content His Mother, changed the water into the best wine. But how was this? As the time for working miracles was that of the public life of Our Lord...yet from all eternity God had determined that nothing that she asked should ever be refused the divine Mother.... That is the sense in which Saint John Chrysostom (+407) understood it; he says that, "Though Jesus answered thus, yet in honor of His Mother He obeyed her request" (*In Jn.*, hom. 21). This is confirmed by St. Thomas Aquinas (+1274), who says that by the words, *My hour is not yet come*, Jesus intended to show, that had the request come from any other, He would not then have complied with it; but because it was addressed to Him by His Mother, He could not refuse it. St. Cyril (+444) and St. Jerome (+420), quoted by Barrada, say the same thing. Also Gaudavensis, on the foregoing passage of St. John, says, that "to honor His Mother, Our Lord anticipated the time for working miracles" (*In Conc. Ev.*, c. 17).

—*St. Alphonsus Liguori, C.SS.R., Bp. C*
Doctor of the Church (+1787)

18. Just as the neck, placed above all other members, passes on to them the vital grace of the head, so also Mary, exalted above all others and presiding over the whole Church, joins the Head to its members. She joins Christ with the Church, and infuses in all its members the life of grace of which she is the primary recipient.

—*St. Amadeus, Cist. (+1159)*

19. Continue, Mary, continue to dispose with confidence of the riches of Your Son; act as Queen, Mother and Spouse of the King: for to you belongs dominion and power over all creatures!

—*Blessed Guerric, Cist.*
Ab. of Igny (+1157)

20. Why did not the mystery of the Incarnation take place without the consent of Mary? Because God wished her to be the beginning of every good.

—*St. Irenaeus, Bp. M.* (+c. 202)

21. Devotion to and love of Most Holy Mary is a great defense, my children, and a powerful weapon against the snare of the Devil.

—*St. John Bosco* (+1888)

22. The History of the Church teaches us that the greatest Saints are those who professed greater devotion to Mary.

—*St. John Bosco* (+1888)

XXX

The Reign of Jesus Through Mary

1.   *Rule you over us, you and your Son.*

—*(Judges 8:22)*

2.   Let the soul of Mary be in each of us to glorify the Lord; let the spirit of Mary be in each of us to rejoice in God.

—*St. Ambrose, Bp. C.*
Doctor of the Church (+397)

3.   That which is given to the Mother redounds to the Son; the honor given to the Queen is honor bestowed on the King.

—*St. Ildephonsus, Bp. C.* (+667)

4.   Our Queen is constantly before the Divine Majesty, interceding for us with her most powerful prayers.

—*Blessed Amadeus, Cist.* (+1159)

5. *The King loved her more than all women, and placed the diadem of His Kingdom on her head* (Esther 2:17). We read that there was a twofold utility in the grace of Esther which she had with the king: one was, that she obtained the royal crown; the other, that she delivered her nation, which had been condemned to death. So Mary, our Esther, obtained such grace with the eternal King that by it she not only attained to the crown herself, but delivered the human race, which was condemned to death. Therefore Saint Anselm (Archbishop of Canterbury, +1109)says: "How shall I worthily praise the Mother of my Lord and God, by whose fecundity I, a captive, was redeemed, by whose Child I, being lost, was recovered and led back from the exile of misery to the homeland of eternal beatitude?"

—*St. Bonaventure, O.F.M., Bp. C.*
Doctor of the Church (+1274)

6. *My power is in Jerusalem* (Ecclus. 24:15). Jerusalem signifies the Church Triumphant in Heaven: it signifies also the Church Militant upon earth. For truly both in Heaven and on earth the Mother of the Creator has power.

—*St. Bonaventure, O.F.M., Bp. C.*
Doctor of the Church (+1274)

7. Let us not imagine, as some do who are misled by erroneous teachings, that Mary, being a creature, is a hindrance to our union with the Creator. It is no longer Mary who lives, it is Jesus Christ, it is God alone Who lives in her. Her transformation into God surpasses that of St. Paul and of the other saints more than the heavens surpass the earth by their height. Mary is made for God alone, and far from ever detaining a soul in herself, she casts the soul upon God and unites it with Him so much the more perfectly as the soul is more perfectly united to her. Mary is the admirable echo of God. When we say "Mary," she answers "God." When with St. Elizabeth, we call her Blessed, she glorifies God. If the falsely enlightened, whom

the devil has so miserably illusioned, even in prayer, had known how to find Mary, and through her to find Jesus, and through Jesus, God the Father, they would not have had such terrible falls. The saints tell us that when we have once found Mary, and through Mary, Jesus, and through Jesus, God the Father, we have found all good.... St. Thomas teaches that in the order of grace, established by Divine Wisdom, God ordinarily communicates Himself to men only through Mary. Therefore, if we would go up to Him and be united with Him, we must use the same means He used to come down to us, to be made man and to impart His graces to us. That means is a true devotion to Our Blessed Lady.

—*St. Louis-Marie Grignon de Montfort* (+1716)

XXXI

Devotion of the Saints to Our Lady

1.   Saints Joachim and Anne earned Divine favor by an irreproachable life and merited that their union should bear for its beautiful fruit the Blessed Virgin Mary, the temple and Mother of God. Joachim, Anne and Mary offered manifestly together a sacrifice of praise to the Holy Trinity. The name of Joachim signifies preparation of the Lord. Is it not he, in fact, who prepares the temple of the Lord, the Blessed Virgin?

—*St. Epiphanius, Ab., Bp. C.* (+403)

2.   Most blessed couple (St. Joachim and St. Anne), the whole creation is in your debt. For it is through you that it has been enabled to offer the Creator a present above all presents, the chaste Mother, who alone was worthy of the Creator. Rejoice, Joachim, for unto us a Son is born of your daughter.

—*St. John Damascene, Pr. C.*
Doctor of the Church (+c. 749)

3. You are the ravisher of hearts: for have you not ravished my heart, O Queen?

—*St. Bernard of Clairvaux, Cist.*
Doctor of the Church (+1153)

4. Hail, my Lady, my Mother; nay, even my heart and my soul.

—*St. Bonaventure, O.F.M., Bp. C.*
Doctor of the Church (+1274)

5. After God, our greatest glory and our greatest joy is Mary.

—*St. Bonaventure, O.F.M., Bp. C.*
Doctor of the Church (+1274)

6. Any devotion, however small, will please Mary, provided it be constant.

—*St. John Berchmans, S.J.* (+1621)

7. Let us love her as did St. Aloysius Gonzaga (S.J., +1581), whose love for Mary burned so unceasingly, that whenever he heard the sweet name of his Mother mentioned, his heart was instantly inflamed and his countenance lighted up with a fire that was visible to all. Let us love as much as St. Francis Solano (O.F.M., +1610), who, maddened as it were—but with a holy madness—with love for Mary, would sing before her picture, and accompany himself on a musical instrument, saying that, like worldly lovers, he serenaded his most sweet Queen.

—*St. Alphonsus Liguori, C.SS.R., Bp. C.*

Doctor of the Church (+1787)

XXXII

Happy Clients of Mary

1.   You, O great Mother, are the beginning, the middle and the end of our happiness.

—*St. Methodius of Olympus* (+c. 311)

2.   Mary not only comes to us when called, but even spontaneously advances to meet us.

—*St. Jerome, Pr. C.*
Doctor of the Church (+420)

3.   O Mother of God, if I place my confidence in you, I shall be saved. If I am under your protection, I have nothing to fear, for the fact of being your client is the possession of a certainty of salvation, which God grants only to those whom He intends to save.

—*St. John Damascene, Pr. C.*
Doctor of the Church (+c. 749)

4.   To serve Mary and to be her courtier is the greatest honor we can possibly possess; for to serve the Queen of Heaven is already to reign there, and to live under her commands is more than to govern.

—*St. John Damascene, Pr. C.*
Doctor of the Church (+c. 749)

5.   As the other planets are illumined by the sun, so do all the elect receive light and increase of happiness from the sight of Mary.

—*St. Bonaventure, O.F.M., Bp. C.*
Doctor of the Church (+1274)

6. *Now all good things come to me together with her, and innumerable riches through her hands* (Wis. 7:11). She is the Mother of all good things, and the world can truly say, that with her (that is, the most Blessed Virgin) it has already received all good things.

—*St. Antoninus, O.P., Bp. C.* (+1459)

7. My children, if you desire perseverance, be devout to Our Blessed Lady.

—*St. Philip Neri* (+1595)

8. Whoever loves Mary will have perseverance.

—*St. John Berchmans, S.J.* (+1621)

9. Oh, what a difference between a soul which has been formed in Christ by the ordinary ways of those who, like the sculptor, trust in their own skill and ingenuity, and a soul thoroughly tractable, entirely detached and well molten, which, without trusting to its own skill, casts itself into Mary, there to be molded by the Holy Ghost! How many stains and defects and illusions, how much darkness and how much human nature is there in the former, and oh, how pure, how heavenly and how Christlike is the latter!

—*St. Louis-Marie Grignon de Montfort* (+1716)

10. Happy, a thousand times happy, is the soul here below to which the Holy Ghost reveals the Secret of Mary in order that it may come to know her; to which He opens the "Garden Enclosed" that it may enter into it; to which He gives access to that "Fountain Sealed" that it may draw from it and drink deep draughts of the living waters of grace!

—*St. Louis-Marie Grignon de Montfort* (+1716)

11. Let the teacher in our order always inculcate all devotion

to the Blessed Virgin, beginning with himself, and he will thus obtain great results, especially in temptations.

—*St. Joseph Calasanctius* (+1648)

12. I am certain of my eternal salvation, of my perseverance in the Society, and of seeing all my designs fulfilled, so long as I love Most Holy Mary.

—*St. John Berchmans, S.J.* (+1621)

XXXIII

Mother of Mercy

1. Mary is so endued with feelings of compassion, that she not only deserves to be called merciful, but even mercy itself.

—*Pope St. Leo the Great*
Doctor of the Church (+461)

2. Mary, by how much she is higher and holier than we are, is more clement and compassionate to converted sinners.

—*Pope St. Gregory the Great*
Doctor of the Church (+604)

3. The higher and more holy she is, the greater is her sweetness and compassion toward sinners, who have recourse with the desire to amend their lives.

—*Pope St. Gregory VII* (+1085)

4. God has ordained that she should assist us in everything.

—*St. Basil the Great, Bp. C.*
Doctor of the Church (+379)

5. By her we obtain the pardon of our sins.

—St. John Chrysostom
Doctor of the Church (+407)

6. Sinners receive pardon by the intercession of Mary alone.

—St. Peter Chrysologus, Bp. C.
Doctor of the Church (+c. 450)

7. The prayers of this Mother have a certain maternal authority with Jesus Christ; so that she obtains the grace of pardon even for those who have been guilty of grievous crimes, and who commend themselves to her.

—St. Germanus of Constantinople, Bp. C. (+c. 732)

8. O Mother of God, your protection never ceases, your intercession is life, and your patronage never fails.

—St. Germanus of Constantinople, Bp. C. (+c.732)

9. Mary stands in the presence of her Son, and never ceases to intercede for sinners.

—St. Bede the Venerable, O.S.B.
Doctor of the Church (+735)

10. Mary is the pledge of Divine mercy.

—St. Andrew of Crete (+720)

11. Open to us the gate of mercy, O holy Mother of God!

—St. John Damascene, Pr. C.
Doctor of the Church (+c. 749)

12. Hear us, loving one; be with us, be favorable to us; help us, most powerful Mother, that our minds may be cleansed from stains and our darkness illuminated.

—St. Anselm, O.S.B., Bp. C.
Doctor of the Church (+1109)

13. If he who prays does not merit to be heard, the merits of the Mother, to whom he recommends himself, will intercede effectually.

—*St. Anselm, O.S.B., Bp. C.*
Doctor of the Church (+1109)

14. In dangers, in troubles, in doubts think of Mary, call upon Mary . . . . If you follow her guidance, you will not go astray. If you pray to her, you will not give up hope. If you think of her, you will not do wrong. If she upholds you, you will not stumble. If she protects you, you will not be afraid. If she leads you, you will reach the goal.

—*St. Bernard of Clairvaux, Cist.*
Doctor of the Church (+1153)

15. We praise her humility, we admire her virginity; but her mercy is sweeter to the unfortunate; we cling more tenderly to her mercy, we remember it more frequently, we invoke it more unceasingly.

—*St. Bernard of Clairvaux, Cist.*
Doctor of the Church (+1153)

16. *A throne shall be prepared in mercy, and one shall sit upon it in truth* (Is. 16:5). The throne of divine mercy is Mary, the Mother of Mercy, in whom all find the solace of mercy . . . . Therefore St. Bernard exultantly says: "Let him be silent on the subject of your mercy, O Blessed Virgin, who, having invoked it in his necessities, found it wanting."

—*St. Bonaventure, O.F.M., Bp. C.*
Doctor of the Church (+1274)

17. Hold in ever highest and most affectionate veneration, the glorious Queen, Mother of Our Lord, turning to her in all your pressing needs and difficulties as to a most sure refuge, imploring the help of her protection, choosing her as your advocate,

whole-heartedly and without misgiving entrusting your cause to her who is the Mother of Mercy, and zealously offering her day by day most special marks of reverence. But that your devotion may be acceptable and your homage pleasing, you must endeavor to maintain within you as best you can, in soul and body, the spotlessness of her purity, and try to your utmost to walk in her footsteps, humbly and gently like her.

—*St. Bonaventure, O.F.M., Bp. C.*
Doctor of the Church (+1274)

18. With the motherhood she by a natural right obtained this dignity in the world, that she is rightly styled the Mother of Mercy. For I find in our King Jesus these two admirable distinctions, namely that He is the eternal God begotten from all eternity, and that he "produces" the eternal God inasmuch as He breathes forth the Holy Spirit. Now, enclosed as He was in the virginal womb, He was nonetheless being generated as the eternal God in eternity by God the Father and nonetheless in the same eternity breathing forth and producing God the Holy Ghost as the Babe in the womb of His Mother. The first distinction, to wit, that He is generated by God, was shared by the Blessed Virgin in so eminent a manner that Jesus is no more truly the Son of God than He is the Son of Mary. And neither greater nor lesser nor more excellent is the Son of God sitting on His Father's throne clothed in brightness than He is wrapped in swaddling clothes and reposing amid the hay in the crib. And that being the dignity of the Mother of the Son of God, Who produces the Holy Spirit, therefore all gifts, virtues and graces of the same Holy Spirit are administered through her hands to whomsoever she wishes, when she wishes, in the way she wishes and in the measure she wishes.

—*St. Bernardine of Siena, O.F.M.* (+1444)

19. The Heart of this good Mother is all love and mercy. She desires only to see us happy. We have only to turn to her to be

heard. The Son has His justice, the Mother has only her mercy.

—*St. Jean-Baptiste-Marie Vianney,*
Cure d'Ars (+1859)

XXXIV

Refuge of Sinners, Comforter of the Afflicted

1. Refuge of sinners: pray for us
    Consoler of the afflicted: pray for us.
    —From the official *Litany of the Blessed Virgin Mary,*
    commonly called *Litany of Loreto*

2. *And God made two great lights: a greater Light to rule the day,*
and a lesser light to rule the night (Gen. 1:16). Whosoever is in the
night of sin, let him cast his eyes on the moon, let him implore
Mary.

—*Pope Innocent III* (+1216)

3. She was predilected for all eternity to be Mother of God,
that those who could not be saved according to the rigor of
Divine Justice, might be so with the help of her sweet mercy and
powerful intercession.

—*St. John Chrysostom*
Doctor of the Church (+407)

4. Mary stands before her Son, unceasingly praying for
sinners.

—*St. Bede the Venerable, O.S.B.*
Doctor of the Church (+735)

5. Mary was raised to the dignity of Mother of God rather for

sinners than for the just, since Jesus Christ declares that He came to call not the just, but sinners.

—*St. Anselm, O.S.B., Bp. C.*
Doctor of the Church (+1109)

6.   It behooves the Queen of Virgins, by a singular privilege of sanctity, to lead a life entirely free from sin, that while she ministered to the Destroyer of death and sin, she should obtain the gift of life and justice for all.

—*St. Bernard of Clairvaux, Cist.*
Doctor of the Church (+1153)

7.   O man, whoever you are, understand that in this world you are tossed about on a stormy and tempestuous sea, rather than walking on solid ground; remember that if you would avoid being drowned, you must never turn your eyes from the brightness of this star, but keep them fixed on it, and call on Mary. In dangers, in straits, in doubts, remember Mary, invoke Mary.

—*St. Bernard of Clairvaux, Cist.*
Doctor of the Church (+1153)

8.   Even when the Mother of God lived in this valley of tears, she was inexpressibly loving and merciful toward the afflicted; how much more compassionate is she now since she reigns happily in Heaven! Now she realizes human misery more fully, and therefore manifests her mercy and assistance more generously. She is, indeed, our Mother; and could a mother forget her children?

—*St. Bonaventure, O.F.M., Bp. C.*
Doctor of the Church (+1274)

9.   When our heart is oppressed with grief and fear and can find no remedy for its suffering, we have no recourse but to look upward to the Queen of Heaven, the Virgin Mary. In every struggle we are sure to find in her both help and consolation. In

truth you are, O Mary, the Mediatrix between sinners and your Divine Son; you are the consoler, the asylum of the afflicted. Turn then and look with pity on me, you who have never turned away your eyes from souls in desolation, for in you is my hope. How many sinners, after abandoning and denying their Lord, losing all hope, have found refuge in you, and, under your protection, returned to God's grace! Divine virtue has made you so kind even to sinners that your goodness restores us to hope. Yes, heaven and earth shall perish before you are seen to abandon the miserable who pray to you sincerely. Truly are you Queen and Mother of Mercy. Rise up, then, and be our Mediatrix to reconcile us to your Divine Son, so that, thanks to you, He may pardon and bring us to eternal life.

—*Blessed Henry Suso, O.P.* (+1365)

10. *I have walked in the waves of the sea* (Ecclus. 24:8). I walk with my servants in the midst of the tempests to which they are constantly exposed (says Our Lady), to assist and preserve them from falling into sin.

—*St. Laurence Justinian* (+1455)

11. If Mary is for us, who shall be against us?

—*St. Antoninus, O.P., Bp. C.* (+1459)

12. As chickens when they see a kite soaring above, run and find refuge under the wings of the hen, so are we preserved under the shadow of your wing. And you, who are our Lady and Mother, have to defend us: for, after God, we have no other refuge than you, who are our only hope and our protectress; towards you we all turn our eyes with confidence.

—*St. Thomas of Villanova, O.S.A.* (+1555)

XXXV

Our Life, Our Sweetness, and Our Hope

1.   *I am the Mother of fair love, and of fear, and of knowledge, and of holy hope.*

—*(Ecclus. 24:24)*

2.   There comes to us the sweet memory of the motherly patronage of the august Queen of Heaven, and we will retain that memory fondly and inviolably with thankful recollection of her favors. From her we derive draughts of heavenly graces as from a teeming channel. In her hands are the treasures of the Lord's mercies. God wishes her to be the source of all blessings.

—*Pope Leo XIII* (+1903)

3.   He who is devout to the Virgin Mother will certainly never be lost.

—*St. Ignatius of Antioch, Bp. M.* (+107)

4.   O Lady, cease not to watch over us; preserve and guard us under the wings of your compassion and mercy, for, after God, we have no hope but in you.

—*St. Ephraem of Edessa*
Doctor of the Church (+373)

5.   O blessed Mary, who can return to you sufficient thanks, or adequately celebrate your praises, for having by your consent succored a ruined world? What praise can human weakness offer to you, which by your means has found the port of salvation? . . . Holy Mary! succor the miserable, help the faint-hearted, comfort the mournful, pray for the people, intercede

for the clergy, pray for the devoted female sex, and let all experience your intercession who celebrate your holy Conception. Amen.

—*From a prayer ascribed to St. Augustine, Bp. C.*
Doctor of the Church (+430)

6.   Whoever could know God, were it not for you, O most holy Mary? Who could be saved? Who would be preserved from dangers? Who would receive any grace, were it not for you, O Mother of God, O full of grace? What hope could we have of salvation, if you did abandon us, O Mary, who are the life of Christians?

—*St. Germanus of Constantinople, Bp. C.* (+c. 732)

7.   O Blessed Mother of God (Deipara), open to us the gate of mercy: for you are the salvation of the human race.

—*St. John Damascene, Pr. C.*
Doctor of the Church (+c. 749)

8.   Let us look more deeply and see with how great a depth of devotion He wishes Mary to be honored by us Who have placed the fullness of all good in Mary, so that if we have any ground for hope, or for salvation, we should know that from her it springs.

—*St. Bernard of Clairvaux, Cist.*
Doctor of the Church (+1153)

9.   *I am the root and stock of David, the bright and Morning Star* (Apoc. 22:16). Mary is called the Star of the Sea: for as those who sail on the ocean are directed to the port they seek by observing the stars, so Christians are directed to glory by Mary.

—*St. Thomas Aquinas, O.P., C.*
Doctor of the Church (+1274)

10. It is impossible that a Mother of God should pray in vain.
—*St. Antoninus, O.P., Bp. C.* (+1459)

XXXVI

Now and at the Hour of Our Death

1.   Grant, we beseech You, O Lord, that we Your servants may enjoy perpetual health of soul and body, and by the glorious intercession of Blessed Mary ever-Virgin, may be delivered from present sorrow and enjoy eternal bliss. Through...
—*A Collect from the Litany of Loreto*

2.   Christian people may piously believe that the Blessed Virgin will help them after death by her continual intercession, her merits, and special protection; and that on Saturdays, the day consecrated by the Church to her, she will in a more particular manner help the souls of the brethren of the Confraternity of Our Blessed Lady of Mount Carmel who have departed this life in a state of grace, provided they have worn the habit, observed the chastity of their state, and recited her Office.
—*Pope Paul V* (+1621)

3.   It is perfectly clear that it is from her that we must look for the grace of a happy death. Indeed, it is even more evident, because the grace of final perseverance is the most important of all graces, inasmuch as it efficaciously consummates the work of everyone's salvation.
—*Pope Benedict XV* (+1922)

4.   Succor me, O Mother of God! O Mother of Mercy! and during my life avert from me the attacks of my enemies, and at

the hour of death preserve my miserable soul, and repel the dark aspects of the devils.

—*St. Epiphanius, Ab., Bp. C.* (+403)

5.   What a day of joy that will be for you, when Mary the Mother of Our Lord, accompanied by the choirs of virgins, will go to meet you!

—*St. Jerome, Pr. C.*
Doctor of the Church (+420)

6.   Through Mary's intercession, many souls are in paradise who would not be there had she not interceded for them, for God has entrusted her with the keys and treasures of the heavenly Kingdom.

—*St. Thomas Aquinas, O.P., C.*
Doctor of the Church (+1274)

7.   Not only does the most Blessed Virgin console and refresh them, but she receives the souls of the dying.

—*St. Vincent Ferrer, O.P., C.* (+1418)

8.   *For in the latter end you shall find rest in her, and she shall be turned to your joy. Then shall her fetters be a strong defense for you, and a firm foundation and her chain a robe of glory. For in her is the beauty of life, and her bands are a healthful binding* (Ecclus. 6: 29-31). O you are indeed fortunate, my brother, if at death you are bound with the sweet chains of the love of the Mother of God! These chains are chains of salvation; they are chains that will insure your eternal salvation, and will make you enjoy in death that blessed peace which will be the beginning of your eternal peace and rest.

—*St. Alphonsus Liguori, C.SS.R., Bp. C.*
Doctor of the Church (+1787)

9. Devotion to Mary is one of the safest means to obtain the grace of a holy death.

—*St. John Bosco* (+1888)

10. Oh, that we may end our lives as did the Capuchin Father, Fulgentius of Ascoli, who expired singing, "O Mary, O Mary, the most beautiful of creatures! let us depart together"; or, according to the annals of the Order, like Blessed Henry the Cistercian, who expired in the very moment that he was pronouncing the most sweet name of Mary.

—*St. Alphonsus Liguori, C.SS.R., Bp. C.*
Doctor of the Church (+1787)

XXXVII

The Most Pure Heart of Mary

1. Almighty and everlasting God, Who in the Heart of the Blessed Virgin Mary did prepare a dwelling worthy of the Holy Ghost: grant in Your mercy, that we who with devout minds celebrate the festival of that Most Pure Heart, may be able to live according to Your own Heart. Through Our Lord...in the unity of the same...

—*A Collect for a Mass of the*
Most Pure Heart of Mary, 22 August

2. No created mind, no created heart, no human force is capable of knowing how much love the Heart of Mary had for Our Lord.

—*St. Jerome, Pr. C.*
Doctor of the Church (+420)

3.   Let us ask Mary to let us be of the number of those whom she carries written on her Heart.

> —*St. Joachima Vedruna de Mas* (+1854)

4.   The love of God had so deeply wounded and penetrated the Heart of Mary, that there was nothing left in it that was not filled with love; for God inflamed no other heart with His love so much as that of the Blessed Virgin. For as she was free from all attachment to earthly things, so she was most susceptible to the flames of this blessed fire.

> —*St. Bernard of Clairvaux, Cist.*
> *Doctor of the Church* (+1153)

5.   Natural love toward Him as her Son, and supernatural love toward Him as her God, were united in the Heart of Mary.

> —*St. Amadeus, Cist.* (+1159)

6.   The bush seen by Moses (Ex. 3:2), which burned without being consumed, was a real symbol of Mary's Heart.

> —*St. Thomas of Villanova, O.S.A.* (+1555)

7.   The Heart of Mary is the heart of the Church Militant, Suffering, and Triumphant.

> —*St. John Eudes, Pr. C.* (+1680)

8.   The Son has His justice, the Mother has nothing but her love, the Heart of Mary.... No grace comes from Heaven without passing through her hands.

> —*St. Jean-Baptiste-Marie Vianney*
> *Cure d'Ars* (+1859)

9.   The Eternal Father takes pleasure in looking upon the Heart of the Most Holy Virgin Mary as the masterpiece of His Hands. The Son takes pleasure in it as the Heart of His Mother,

the source from which He drew the blood that ransomed us. The Holy Ghost dwells in Mary as in His temple.

—*St. Jean-Baptiste-Marie Vianney*
Cure d'Ars (+1859)

10. The Heart of Mary is so tender towards us, that the hearts of all mothers in the world put together cannot be compared to hers. All that the Son asks the Father is granted Him. All that the Mother asks of the Son is in like manner granted to her.

—*St. Jean-Baptiste-Marie Vianney*
Cure d'Ars (+1859)

11. Those who would know the intimate secrets of Divine Love and the hidden virtues of Jesus' Divinity, must study them in the transparent mirror of the Immaculate Heart of Mary.

—*St. Peter Julien Eymard* (+1868)

12. As the Church and the entire human race were consecrated to the Sacred Heart of Jesus so that, in reposing all hope in Him, He might become for them the sign and pledge of victory and salvation; so we in like manner consecrate ourselves forever also to your Immaculate Heart, Our Mother and Queen, that your love and patronage may hasten the triumph of the Kingdom of God and that all nations, at peace with one another and with God, may proclaim you blessed and with you raise their voices to resound from pole to pole in the chant of the everlasting Magnificat of glory, love and gratitude to the Heart of Jesus, where they can find truth and peace.

—*Pope Pius XII* (+1958)

XXXVIII

Neglect of Our Lady

1.   With what shameless boldness do they attack that stainless Virgin, who merited to be the dwelling-place of God; who out of the infinite number of Israelites was elected for this one end, that she might be consecrated as the vessel and habitation for the Divine Childbirth.

—St. Epiphanius, Ab., Bp. C. (+403)

2.   Not only those, O Lady, offend you who outrage you, but you are also offended by those who neglect to ask your favors.

—St. Bonaventure, O.F.M., Bp. C.
Doctor of the Church (+1274)

XXXIX

The Imitation of Mary

1.   There is nothing by which we can with greater certainty gain the affection of Mary than by charity toward our neighbor.

—St. Gregory Nazianzen
Doctor of the Church (+390)

2.   *Now, therefore, children, hear me; blessed are they that keep my ways* (Prov. 8:32). Mary was such that her life alone was a model for all. Let the virginity and life of Mary be to you as a faithful image, in which the form of virtue is resplendent.

Thence learn how to live, what to correct, what to avoid, what to retain.

—*St. Ambrose, Bp. C.*
Doctor of the Church (+397)

3. He who does not the works of his Mother, abjures his lineage. Mary humble, and he proud; Mary pure, and he wicked; Mary full of love, and he hating his neighbor.

—*St. Peter Chrysologus, Bp. C.*
Doctor of the Church (+c. 450)

4. Serve Mary, whom you love; for you then truly love her, if you endeavor to imitate her whom you love.

—*St. Sophronius* (+c. 640)

5. If you cannot imitate the virginity of this humble Virgin, imitate her humility.

—*St. Bernard of Clairvaux, Cist.*
Doctor of the Church (+1153)

XL

The Holy Rosary

1. By the Rosary the darkness of heresy has been dispelled, and the light of the Catholic Faith shines with all its brilliancy.

—*Pope St. Pius V* (+1572)

2. Urban IV (+1264) testifies that "every day the Rosary obtains fresh boons for Christianity." Sixtus IV (+1484) declared that this method of prayer "redounded to the honor of God and the Blessed Virgin, and was well suited to obviate dangers," and Leo X (+1521), that "it was instituted to oppose pernicious heresiarchs and heresies"; while Julius III (+1555)

called it "the glory of the Church." St. Pius V (+1572) said that "with the spread of this devotion, the meditations of the Faithful have begun to be more ardent and their prayers more fervent."

—Pope Leo XIII (+1903)

3.   To the honor of Mary, the great Mother of God, for a perpetual remembrance of the prayer for her protection offered among all nations throughout the month of October to her Most Pure Heart; as an enduring testimony of the unbounded trust which we put in our most loving Mother, and in order that we may day by day more and more obtain her favorable aid: we will and decree that in the Litany of Loreto, after the invocation, "Queen conceived without original sin," shall be added the suffrage, "Queen of the most Holy Rosary, pray for us."

—Pope Leo XIII (+1903)

4.   In the Rosary, along with the most beautiful and efficacious prayers arranged in an orderly pattern, the chief mysteries of our religion follow one another, brought before our mind for contemplation: first of all the mysteries in which the Word was made flesh and Mary, the inviolate Virgin and Mother, performs her maternal duties for Him with a holy joy; there come then the sorrows, the agony and death of the suffering Christ, the price at which the salvation of our race was accomplished; then follow the mysteries full of His glory, His triumph over death, the Ascension into Heaven, the sending of the Holy Spirit, the resplendent brightness of Mary received among the stars, and finally the everlasting glory of all the Saints in Heaven united with the glory of the Mother and her Son.

—Pope Leo XIII (+1903)

5.   The formula of the Rosary is excellently adapted to prayer in common, so that it has been styled, not without reason, "The Psalter of Mary." That old custom of our forefathers ought to

be preserved or restored, whereby Christian families, whether
in town or country, used to gather piously at the close of the
day, when their labors were at an end, before a representation
of Our Lady and alternately recite the Rosary. She, delighted at
this faithful unanimous homage, was ever near them like a
loving mother surrounded by her children, distributing to them
the blessings of domestic peace, the foretaste of the peace of
Heaven.

—*Pope Leo XIII* (+1903)

6. The history of the Church bears testimony to the power
and efficacy of this form of prayer (the Rosary) recording as
it does the rout of the Turkish forces at the naval battle of
Lepanto, and the victories gained over the same in the last
century at Temesvar in Hungary, and on the island of Corfu.
Our predecessor, Gregory XIII (+1585), in order to perpetuate
the memory of the first-named victory, established the feast of
Our Lady of Victories, which Clement XI (+1721) later dis-
tinguished by the title of Rosary Sunday (the Feast of the Holy
Rosary was subsequently changed from a movable, first Sunday
of October, to the fixed date, 7 October) and commanded it to
be celebrated throughout the universal Church.

—*Pope Leo XIII* (+1903)

7. The Roman Pontiffs have ever given the highest praise to
this (Rosary) Confraternity of Our Lady. Innocent VIII
(+1492) calls it "a most devout confraternity." St. Pius V
(+1572) declares that by its virtue "Christians began suddenly
to be transformed into other men, the darkness of heresy to be
dispelled, and the light of Catholic faith to shine forth". . . . Of
late the beautiful devotion to our Blessed Mother called "the
Living Rosary" has once more become popular. We have gladly
blessed this devotion, and we . . . cherish the strongest hope that
these prayers and praises, rising incessantly from the lips and
hearts of so great a multitude, will be most efficacious. Alternately rising by night and day throughout the different coun-

tries of the earth, they combine a harmony of vocal prayer with meditation upon the divine mysteries.

—*Pope Leo XIII* (+1903)

8.   Father and mother of families particularly must give an example to their children, especially when, at sunset, they gather together after the day's work, within the domestic walls, and recite the Holy Rosary on bended knees before the image of the Virgin, together fusing voice, faith and sentiment. This is a beautiful and salutary custom, from which certainly there cannot but be derived tranquillity and abundance of heavenly gifts for the household.

—*Pope Pius XI* (+1939)

9.   Nor are there lacking men famous as to doctrine and wisdom who, although intensely occupied in scientific study and researches, never even for a day fail to pray fervently, on bended knee, before the image of the Virgin, in this most pious form. Thus kings and princes, however burdened with the most urgent occupations and affairs, made it their duty to recite the Rosary. This mystic crown, then, not only is found in and glides through the hands of the poor, but it also is honored by citizens of every social rank.

—*Pope Pius XI* (+1939)

XLI

Our Lady and Sacred Scripture

1.   She was foretold by the Prophets, foreshadowed in types and figures by the Patriarchs, described by the Evangelists, saluted most courteously by the Angels.

—*St. Sophronius* (+c. 640)

2. In you is the curse of Adam done away, and the debt of Eve is paid. You are the Ark of Noe and the bond (rainbow) of reconciliation with God in a new generation. You are the exceeding glory of the kingdom and priesthood of Melchisedech; you are the unshaken trust of Abraham, the burnt offering of Isaac. You are the Ladder that Jacob saw going up to Heaven, and the most noble of all his children. O purest! you are the book of Moses, the law-giver, whereon the New Covenant is written with the finger of God. You are Aaron's rod that budded. You are as David's daughter, all glorious within, wrought about with divers colors. Hail! just hope of the Patriarchs. Hail! special honor of all the Saints.

—*St. Tarasius, Patriarch of Constantinople* (+806)

3. You, O Mary, are the vessel and chamber containing all mysteries. You know what the Patriarchs never knew; you have experienced what was never revealed to the Angels; you have heard what the Prophets never heard. In a word, all that was hidden from preceding generations was made manifest to you; even more, most of these wonders were dependent on you.

—*St. Gregory Thaumaturgus, Bp. C.* (+c. 270)

4.   *From Ecclesiasticus*

He poured her out upon all His works,
and upon all flesh according to His gift,
and has given her to them that love Him...

They that serve her, shall be servants to the Holy One:
and God loves them that love her...

Come to her with all your mind
and keep her ways with all your power.

Search for her, and she shall be made known to you,
and when you have gotten her, let her not go:

For in the latter end you shall find rest in her,
and she shall be turned to joy...

And in the midst of her own people she shall be exalted,
and shall be admired in the holy assembly.

And in the multitude of the elect she shall have praise,
and among the blessed she shall be Blessed, saying:
I came out of the mouth of the Most High,
the first-born before all creatures...
Then the Creator of all things commanded, and said to me;
and He that made me rested in my tabernacle.
And he said to me: Let your dwelling be in Jacob,
and your inheritance in Israel,
and take root in my elect.
From the beginning, and before the world, was I created,
and unto the world to come I shall not cease to be,
and in the holy dwelling-place I have ministered before
    Him.
And so was I established in Sion,
and in the holy city likewise I rested,
and my power was in Jerusalem...
and my abode is in the full assembly of Saints...
I am the Mother of fair love, and of fear,
and of knowledge, and of holy hope.
In me is all grace of the way and of the truth,
in me is all hope of life and of virtue...
They that explain me shall have life everlasting.
For her thoughts are more vast than the sea,
and her counsels more deep than the great ocean.

—*Excerpts from the Book of Sirach*

XLII

Our Lady and the Liturgy

1.   *Stabat Mater Dolorosa*
                    At the Cross her station keeping,
                    Stood the mournful Mother weeping,
                        Close to Jesus at the last:

Through her Heart, His sorrow sharing,
All His bitter anguish bearing,
   Now at length the sword has passed.
Oh, how sad and sore distressed
Was that Mother highly blest
   Of that sole-begotten One!
Christ above in torment hangs;
She beneath beholds the pangs
   Of her dying glorious Son.

Is there one who would not weep,
Whelmed in miseries so deep,
   Christ's dear Mother to behold?
Can the human heart refrain
From partaking in her pain,
   In that Mother's pain untold?
Bruised, derided, cursed, defiled,
She beheld her tender Child
   All with bloody scourges rent;
For the sins of His own nation,
Saw Him hang in desolation,
   Till His spirit forth He sent.

O thou Mother! fount of love!
Touch my spirit from above,
   Make my heart with thine accord;
Make me feel as thou hast felt;
Make my soul to glow and melt
   With the love of Christ my Lord.
Holy Mother! pierce me through;
In my heart each wound renew
   Of my Savior crucified:
Let me share with thee His pain,
Who for all my sins was slain,
   Who for me in torments died.

Let me mingle tears with thee,
Mourning Him Who mourned for me,
   All the days that I may live:

By the Cross with thee to stay;
There with thee to weep and pray,
   Is all I ask of thee to give.
Virgin of all virgins blest!
Listen to my fond request:
   Let me share thy grief divine;
Let me, to my latest breath,
In my body bear the death
   Of that dying Son of thine.

Wounded with His every wound,
Steep my soul till it hath swooned
   In His very Blood away;
Be to me, O Virgin, nigh,
Lest in flames I burn and die,
   In that awful Judgment day.

Christ, when Thou shalt call me hence,
Be Thy Mother my defense,
   Be Thy Cross my victory;
While my body here decays,
May my soul Thy goodness praise,
   Safe in Paradise with Thee.
      —*Blessed Jacopone da Todi, O.F.M.* (+1306)

2.   *Quem terra, pontus, sidera*

The God Whom earth, and sea, and sky
Adore, and laud, and magnify,
Who o'er their three-fold fabric reigns,
The Virgin's spotless womb contains.

The God, Whose will by moon and sun
And all things in due course is done,
Is borne upon a Maiden's breast,
By fullest heavenly grace possessed.

How blest that Mother, in whose shrine
The great Artificer Divine,
Whose hand contains the earth and sky,
Vouchsafed, as in His ark, to lie.

Blest, in the message that Gabriel brought;
Blest, by the work the Spirit wrought;
From Whom the Great Desire of earth
Took human flesh and human birth.

All honor, laud and glory be,
O Jesu, Virgin-born, to Thee;
All glory, as is ever meet,
To Father and to Paraclete.

—*Ascribed to St. Venantius Fortunatus* (+609)

O gloriosa Virginum

3.   O glorious Lady! throned on high
Above the star-illumined sky;
Thereto ordained, thy bosom lent
To thy Creator nourishment.

Through thy sweet Offspring we receive
The bliss once lost through hapless Eve;
And Heaven to mortals open lies
Now thou art Portal of the skies.

Thou art the door of Heaven's high King,
Light's Gateway fair and glistening;
Life through a Virgin is restored;
Ye ransomed nations, praise the Lord!

—*Ascribed usually to St. Venantius Fortunatus* (+609),
or to St. Anthony of Padua, O.F.M.
Doctor of the Church (+1231)

4.   You, O daughter, are blessed of the Lord, for through you
have we been partakers of the Fruit of Life.

—*An Antiphon for Lauds*
Office of the B. V. Mary

5.   O Blessed Virgin Mary, you are the channel of pardon, you
are the Mother of Grace, you are the hope of the world: gra-

ciously hear your children who cry unto you.

—*An Antiphon for Vespers*
Feast of Our Mother of Grace

6.   O Holy Mary, be you a help to the helpless, a strength to the fearful, a comfort to the sorrowful; pray for the people, plead for the clergy, make intercession for all women vowed to God; may all that keep your holy rememberance feel the might of your assistance.

—*An Antiphon for Sunday Vespers*

7.   May the holy intercession of Your glorious Mother Mary, ever-Virgin, help us, O Lord, we beseech You; and may those on whom she has bestowed blessings unto eternal life be delivered from all danger and become united by her loving kindness. Who lives...

—*A Postcommunion for the Feast of*
Our Lady of Mount Carmel, 16 July

8.   May the humanity of Your only-begotten Son be our succor, O Lord, that He, Who, born of a Virgin, did not diminish but hallowed the integrity of His Mother, may on this festival of her Nativity, deliver us from our sins, and make our offerings acceptable to You. Who...

—*A Secret for the Mass on the*
Nativity, B. V. Mary, 8 Sept.

9. Through Your mercy, O Lord, and by the intercession of Blessed Mary ever-Virgin, Mother of Your only-begotten Son, may this oblation secure for us present and perpetual prosperity and peace. Through the same Lord...

—*A Secret for the Feast of the*
Maternity, B. V. Mary, 11 October

10. To Your faithful people, rejoicing in the name and protec-

tion of the most holy Virgin Mary, vouchsafe, Almighty God, we beseech You, through her loving intercession, to be delivered from all evils here on earth, and to be accounted worthy to enter into everlasting joys in Heaven. Through...

—*A Collect for the Feast of the*
Most Holy Name of Mary, 12 September

11. May the right hand of Your Immaculate Mother raise up those, O Lord, whom You have fed plenteously with Food from Heaven, that through her help we may come to our everlasting home. Who lives...

—*A Postcommunion for the Feast of the*
Apparition of Our Lady at Lourdes, 11 February

12. O Lord Jesus Christ, our Mediator with the Father, Who has appointed the most Blessed Virgin, Your Mother, to be our Mother also and our Mediatrix before You: grant that whosoever draws near to You to beseech any benefit, may receive all things through her and rejoice. Who lives and reigns...

—*A Collect for the Feast of the B. V. Mary*
Mediatrix of All Graces, 31 May

13. Refreshed by these Divine Gifts, we humbly beseech You, O Lord, that by the intercession of the blessed Virgin Mary the solemn feast of whose Most Pure Heart we now celebrate, we may be delivered from present dangers, and obtain the joys of everlasting life. Through our Lord...

—*A Postcommunion for the Feast of the*
Most Pure Heart of Mary, 22 August

14. Return through your power: He that is mighty has done unto you great things, and all power is given to you in Heaven and on earth: nothing is impossible with you, with whom it is possible to raise up the hopeless unto the hope of blessedness. For how could that Power withstand your power, Whose flesh

sprang of your flesh? You draw near unto the golden altar of man's Atonement, not praying only, but bidding, not as a hand-maid, but as a Lady. Be moved by your nature, be moved by your power. The mightier you are, so much more ought you to be merciful. Return through love, Lady! I know that you are most kind, and that you love with an unconquered love us whom your Son and your God loved with the highest love, in you and through you. Who knows how often you cool the anger of the Judge when the might of justice is going forth from before God?

—*A Lesson from Matins*
Feast of Our Mother of the Divine Shepherd
First Sunday in May

15.   Rejoice, O Mary, by whose mighty hand
      The Church hath victory o'er Her foes achieved,
      Since thou to Gabriel's word of quickening power
      In lowliness has listened, and believed—
      Thou, still a Virgin, in thy blessed womb
      Hast God Incarnate of thy flesh conceived,
      And still of Heaven, of that virginity
      Remainest after childbirth unbereaved.

—*A Responsory for Matins*
Feast of the Annunciation, 25 March

16. Through you, O Mother of God, has the life we had lost been given back to us: for, from Heaven receiving Him Who became your Son, you on the world have bestowed its Savior. Alleluia.

—*From a Gradual for the*
Feast of Our Lady of Mount Carmel, 16 July

17. Be mindful, O Virgin Mother, to speak good things before

God's face in our behalf, so that He may turn away His anger from us.

—An Offertory (cf. Jer. 18:20)
Feast of Our Lady of Mount Carmel

18. Most worthy Queen of the world, Mary, ever Virgin, pray for our peace and safety: you who did bring forth Christ the Lord and Savior of all mankind.

—A Communion prayer for the Feast of
Our Lady of Mount Carmel, 16 July

19. O God, Who by having in a special manner placed us under the partonage of the most blessed Virgin Mary, has been pleased to heap unceasing favors on us: grant to us, your suppliants, whose joy it is this day to honor her on earth, forevermore to be made happy by seeing her in Heaven.

—A Collect for the Feast of
Our Lady of Guadalupe, 12 December

20. Through Your indulgent mercy, O Lord, and through the prayers of Blessed Mary ever a Virgin, may this oblation avail to the ensuring to us of prosperity and peace, now and there forevermore.

—A Secret for the Feast of
Our Lady of Guadalupe, 12 December

21. Give unto us, O Lord, who have received these helps to salvation, to find, wheresoever we may be, a sure defense in the patronage of Blessed Mary ever a Virgin: for it is her honor that, humbly, we have made in our offerings to Your Divine Majesty. Through...

—A Postcommunion for the Feast of

Our Lady of Guadalupe, 12 December

22. O Lord Almighty, Who has willed that all things should be given to us through the Immaculate Mother of Your Son: grant that under the protection of this mighty Mother, we may escape all the dangers of these our times, and in the end may come to life everlasting. Through...

—A Postcommunion for the Feast of
Our Lady of the Miraculous Medal, 27 November

23. May, at all times, O Lord, the venerable intercession of Your glorious Mother, Mary ever-Virgin, be our hope. She has loaded us with everlasting gifts: may she ever make us to see what it behooves us to do, and may she strengthen us to be the fulfilling thereof.

—A Postcommunion for the Feast of
Our Lady of Good Counsel, 26 April

24. O God, Who by means of the most glorious Mother of Your Son was pleased to give new children to Your Church for the deliverance of Christ's faithful from the power of the heathen: grant, we beseech You, that we who love and honor her as the foundress of so great a work may, by her merits and intercession, be ourselves delivered from all sin and from the bondage of the evil one. Through the same Lord...

—A Collect for the Feast of
Our Lady of Ransom, 24 September

Some Prayers to Our Lady from Eastern Catholic Liturgies:
25. How can I praise you duly, O most chaste Virgin? For you alone among men are all holy, and you give to all the help and grace they need. All we who are on earth put our hope in you: strengthen our faith, shine through the dimness of this world, while we, children of the Church, sing in your praise. Throne of the cherubim are you and gate of Heaven: pray without ceasing for us, that we may be saved in the day of dread. Amen.

—Antiochene Syriac Rite

26. Let your intercession be with us, O Mother most pure, and come to us in our need as is your wont. We are exiles on this earth, without end ever before our eyes, and even now many of us perish: help us by your prayers, O merciful Maiden, and be always our advocate lest we are lost through our own ill will. Blessed and most holy one, plead for us before God, that He may be pitiful to us through your asking. Amen.

—Maronite (Antiochene) Rite

27. O Mother of God, trusting in you we shall not be ashamed but saved. Strengthened by your help and intercession, O holy, pure and perfect one, we shall resist our temptations and scatter them. We take up the shelter of your aid as a strong shield, and we supplicate you, O Mother of God, that you preserve us through your prayers. Lead us out of the darkness of sin to glorify the Almighty God Who took flesh in you. Amen.

—Coptic Office of Sleep, Alexandrian Rite

28. On account of the great multitude of my transgressions, I come to you, O Mother of God, asking for salvation. Visit you my ailing soul, and beseech your Son and our God to grant me remission of the sins I have committed, O you most Blessed One.

—From the Office of Communion Preparation,
according to Greek Rite

29. *The Hail Mary, as said in the Abyssinian Liturgy:*

Hail Mary, full of grace, the Lord is with you; blessed are you among women and blessed is the fruit of your womb. Pray and intercede with your beloved Son that He forgive us our sins.

30. *The Hail Mary, in Old-Slavonic (Byzantine) Rite:*

Hail, Mother of God, Virgin Mary, full of grace, the Lord is with you; blessed are you among women, and blessed is the fruit of your womb. For you have borne Christ, the Savior and Deliverer of our souls.

31. *Some Bohorodichens (hymns of Our Lady) from the Old-Slavonic Byzantine Rite:*

Your mysteries are above understanding and most glorious, O Mother of God, for, spotless and virgin, you are acknowledged a true Mother, and have borne the true God: pray to Him that He save our souls.

We praise you, O Virgin Mother of God, who *did mediate the salvation of our race*; for your Son and our God, by the flesh received from you, endured passion and as lover of mankind delivered us from corruption.

Hail, impassable gate of the Lord! Hail, bulwark and protection of those who fly to you! Hail, untroubled haven and Virgin, who has borne in flesh your Creator and God. Do not cease to pray for those who laud and reverence your childbearing.

As the treasure of our resurrection, do you, O universally celebrated Virgin, raise those hoping in you from the pit and depth of sin; for you have saved the repentant from sin, having borne our Salvation, and was before bearing Virgin, in bearing Virgin and after bearing remained Virgin.

Some Tropars (hymns for special feasts) from the Old-Slavonic Byzantine Rite:

32.   Your Nativity, O Virgin Mother of God, has proclaimed joy throughout the whole world, for from you the Sun of Righteousness, Christ our God, has shone, Who has destroyed the curse and given blessings, laid death aside and gave us eternal life.

—*Nativity B. V. Mary,*
8 September, Julian Calendar

33.   We, faithful, hold a joyful feast today, shadowed by your coming. O Mother of God, and looking upon your most holy

image, we reverently say: cover us with your severed veil and liberate us from all evil, beseeching your Son, Christ our God, to save our souls.

—Protection of the Blessed Virgin, 1 October

34. Today is the beginning of our salvation and manifestation of the mystery that was from eternity, the Son of God becoming the Son of the Virgin, while Gabriel announces the grace; wherefore let us also say with him to the Mother of God: hail, gracious one, the Lord is with you.

—Annunciation, 25 March

35. To you, O Mother of God, the chosen Guide, your servants sing a triumphal hymn, rendering you thanks for deliverance from evils; and since you have invincible power, deliver us, we beseech you, from all ill, that we may cry to you, hail, immaculate bride.

—Kondak, tone 8
Feast of Annunciation

36. Meet indeed it is to bless you, Mother of God, ever blessed and most sinless Mother of Our God. Honored above the cherubim, infinitely more glorious than the seraphim, who did bear God the Word and are still Maiden. Mother of God in truth, you we magnify.

—Hymn of Praise, from the
Liturgy of St. John Chrysostom

37. O full of grace, all creation, the angelic host and the race of men, rejoices in you: holy sanctuary, spiritual paradise, glory of virgins from whom God took flesh; He Who was God before all time became a little Child within you. Your lap was His throne, and your womb He made greater than the sky. All creatures are joyful in you, O full of grace. Glory to you.

—Hymn of Praise, from
Byzantine Liturgy of St. Basil

38. Mother of God, gateway of Heaven to men,
    with a divine voice the angel declared:
        Hail, full of grace, the Lord is with thee.
    He Who sitteth with the Father above the cherubim
    was pleased to dwell within thy maiden body,
        Hail, full of grace, the Lord is with thee.
    He Who dwelt amid the flaming seraphim
    was seen among men and in a creature's arms;
        Hail, full of grace, the Lord is with thee.

                                    —*Hymn from the Armenian Ritual*

XLIII

Our Lady and the Liturgical Year

1. Hail, most pure Virgin.
    Hail, honorable sceptre of Christ the King.
    Hail, mysteriously growing cluster.
    Hail, gate of Heaven and unburned bush.
    Hail, universal light. Hail, joy of all.
    Hail, salvation of the faithful.
    Hail, mediatrix of all Christians.
    Hail, glory of the universe. Hail, temple of the Lord.
    Hail, overshadowing mountain.
    Hail, refuge of all. Hail, golden light.
    Hail, pious glory of the truly faithful.
    Hail, Mary, Mother of Christ God.
    Hail, paradise.
    Hail, divine altar. Hail, sanctuary.
    Hail, ever golden hand. Hail, hope of all.

                                    —*Sticheras from the*
                                    Paraklis service in honor of
                                    Mary, Old-Slavonic Rite

XLIV

Our Lady and the Holy Eucharist

1.   Through the prayers of Your pure Mother, the Blessed ever-Virgin Mary, my sure hope and protection, enable me without condemnation to partake of Your holy, immortal, life-giving and terrible Mysteries....

—*St. John Chrysostom*
Doctor of the Church (+407)

2.   It is through Mary that we are able to eat the Bread of Heaven every day; it is through her prayers that God inspires us to receive It and grants us the grace to receive It worthily. As Eve induced man to eat of the forbidden fruit which brought death upon us, so it is right that Mary should prompt us to eat the Bread which gives us life.

—*St. Peter Damian, Bp. C.*
Doctor of the Church (+1072)

XLV

Mediatrix of All Graces

1.   *In me is all grace of the way and of the truth.*

—*(Ecclus. 24:25)*

2.   O Lord Jesus Christ, our Mediator with the Father, Who has been pleased to appoint the most Blessed Virgin Your Mother, to be our Mother also, and our Mediatrix with You, mercifully grant that whosoever comes to You seeking Your

favors may rejoice to receive all of them through her.
                              —*A Prayer from the Office of Our Lady,*
                                   Mediatrix of All Graces (31 May)

3.   Rest assured that the purer your words and your glances
are, the more you will please the Virgin Mary, and the greater
the graces that she will obtain for you from her divine Son.
                              —*St. John Bosco* (+1888)

4.   No shepherdess has as much care of her sheep, as does
Most Holy Mary of the souls entrusted to her care.
                              —*St. Anthony Mary Claret, Bp. C.* (+1870)

5.   Mary is Daughter of God the Father, Mother of God the
Son, Spouse of God the Holy Spirit, temple and shrine of the
Most Holy Trinity.
                              —*St. Anthony Mary Claret, Bp. C.* (+1870)

6.   Once conceived the divine plan of the Incarnation of the
Word, for the redemption and glorification of humankind,
Mary became an integral part of it, as destined to provide a
human body for the Redeemer.
                              —*St. Anthony Mary Claret, Bp. C.* (+1870)

7.   In imitation of Jesus, a Christian should love Mary, and
think the best of her. He should have her for mother, and as
such love her, serve her, wait upon her, and, like Jesus, be
totally subject to her.
                              —*St. Anthony Mary Claret, Bp. C.* (+1870)

8.   Mary is the heart of the Church. From this heart, there
spring out continuously all the works of charity.
                              —*St. Anthony Mary Claret, Bp. C.* (+1870)

9.   It was because he was "born of woman" (Gal. 4:4) that

Our Lord Jesus Christ makes us real "adopted sons" (cf. *Lumen Gentium*, n. 52). It was because she received the word of God both in her heart and in her body that the Blessed Virgin has a unique role in the mystery of the Word incarnate and in that of the Mystical Body. She is closely united with the Church, for which she is the model of faith, charity and perfect union with Christ. In this way, in answer to our devotion and our prayer, Mary, who in a way gathers and reflects in herself the highest aspirations of faith, calls the faithful to her Son and to his Sacrifice, as well as to the love of the Father.

—Pope John Paul II

10. When I remember all the graces I have received from God through Mary, it seems to me that I am like one of those churches in which a miraculous image of the Madonna is venerated, the walls of which are covered with votive offerings inscribed: *For a grace received from Mary.* Yes, there is nothing I have on which I cannot write: *A grace received through Mary.*

—St. Leonard of Port Maurice, O.F.M. (+1751)

11. We offer our praise to the Most Pure and Most Holy Virgin Mary, for it is from her and by her that there flow down upon us heavenly graces greater than heart can conceive: she is the torrent of Divine Goodness.

—Greek Menology
Feast of St. Theophanes, 17 January, Od. 21.

12. Lord God Almighty, You have willed that we should have all things through the Immaculate Mother of Your Son; grant them....

—A Postcommunion for the
Feast of the Miraculous Medal
27 November, Roman Missal

13. Most merciful God, to procure the salvation of sinners and

to provide a refuge for the unfortunate, You have ordained
that the Virgin Mary should be the Mother of Your only Son
and the Almoner of His graces; grant then, we beseech You . . .

—A Collect for the Feast of the
Immaculate Heart of Mary
Refuge of Sinners, in
Supplement to Roman Missal for Paris

14. Mary is as it were the heavenly canal by which the waters
of all graces and gifts flow down into the souls of wretched
human beings.

—Pope Benedict XIV (+1758)

15. The most sure refuge and never-failing security in the
midst of all dangers, the most powerful Mediatrix and Advocate of the whole world with her only Son.

—Pope Pius IX (+1878)

16. The Virgin Mother is the Mediatrix of our peace with God,
and the Almoner of heavenly graces. She has entered into the
highest state of power and glory in Heaven in order that she may
accord the help of her patronage to men in their journey
through so many distresses and perils to the happy City. . . .
God chose her to be His Mother and by that very choice has
associated her with Himself in the work of the salvation of men.

—Pope Leo XIII (+1903)

17. God has made the Virgin Mother Almoner of Heavenly
Graces. May God . . . graciously hear at long last the prayers of
those who turn in supplication to Him, through her whom He
Himself has willed to be the Almoner of Heavenly Graces.

—Pope Leo XIII (+1903)

18. In a true and natural sense may we say that from the great

treasury of graces that the Lord has merited for us, nothing came to us, except through Mary.

—*Pope Leo XIII* (+1903)

19. Of the magnificent treasure of grace brought us by Christ, nothing, according to the eternal designs, is to be distributed to us except through Mary. Hence, it is through her we must go to Christ, almost in the same way as through Christ we approach our Heavenly Father.

—*Pope Leo XIII* (+1903)

20. The recourse we have to Mary in prayer follows upon the office she uninterruptedly fills by the side of the throne of God as Mediatrix of Divine Grace, being by worthiness and by merit most acceptable to Him, and for that reason surpassing in power all the angels and saints in Heaven.

—*Pope Leo XIII* (+1903)

21. Mary is our Mediatrix with our Mediator.

—*Pope Leo XIII* (+1903)

22. The cataracts of Divine Grace pour down upon us from Mary as through an overflowing channel. As St. Peter Damian has said, "In her hands are the treasures of the Divine Mercies" (*Serm. I de Nat. Virg.*). God wishes her to be the source of all that is good.

—*Pope Leo XIII* (+1903)

23. Far be it from us to attribute to the Mother of God the power of producing supernatural grace, for this power belongs to God alone. But, because she outstrips all other creatures in holiness, and in the intimacy of her union with Christ, and because she has been, according to the Divine Plan, associated with Christ in the work of Redemption, she has merited by a merit of fitness all that Christ has merited by a merit of justice

and God has constituted her the Almoner of His Graces.

—*Pope St. Pius* X (+1914)

24. She is the dispensatrix of the graces that Jesus Christ has merited for us by His Blood and His death.

—*Pope St. Pius* X (+1914)

25. Our sight of Christ (the Prince of Peace) born for us is made complete by our sight of Mary, in whom the faith of believers, and the love of sons recognize not only the Queen of Peace, but the Mediatrix between rebellious man and the merciful God. She is the *aurora pacis rutilans* across the darkness of this world.... When man has hardened his own heart, and his hates have overrun the earth; when fire and sword are raging, and when the world rings with the sound of weeping and the noise of arms; when human reason is found at fault, and all civilized rights are scattered like thistledown, faith and history alike point us to the one succor, to the omnipotence of prayer, to the Mediatrix, to Mary.

—*Pope Benedict* XV (+1922)

26. It has pleased God to grant us all graces through the intercession of Mary.... All the graces which the Giver of all good deigns to grant to the descendants of Adam, are dispensed to us, in the disposition of a loving Providence, through the hands of the Blessed Virgin.... The graces of all kinds that we receive from the treasury of the Redemption are dispensed by the hands of the Sorrowful Virgin.

—*Pope Benedict* XV (+1922)

27. All graces which come to us from the treasury of the Redemption are, by reason of her cooperation, distributed to us by the Sorrowful Virgin.

—*Pope Benedict* XV (+1922)

28. Everything comes to us from Almighty God through the hands of Our Lady.

—*Pope Pius XI* (+1939)

29. Now that the situation is worse, and that this terrible war has broken out, bringing with it already untold harm and suffering, we cannot but call again on our children scattered throughout the world to gather around the altar of the Virgin Mother of God daily during the month consecrated to her, to offer her suppliant prayer.... And since, as St. Bernard says, "It is the will of God that we should obtain all through Mary," all should have recourse to her.... The Blessed Virgin is in fact so powerful with God that, as Dante sings,

"...he who grace desireth, and comes not
To thee for guidance, fain would have desire to
Fly without wings."

—*Pope Pius XII* (+1958)

30. It becomes you, as being Mother of God, Queen, Lady and Mistress, for the sake of the King, Lord God and Master, born of you, to be mindful of us, as you stand near Him Who...granted you all graces, whence you are called "full of grace."... Be mindful of us, most Holy Virgin, and bestow on us gifts from the riches of your graces, O you, full of grace.

—*St. Athanasius, Bp. C.*
Doctor of the Church (+373)

31. Most Holy Lady, Mother of God, full of grace, our nature's glory, channel of all good things, Queen of all things after the Trinity, Mediatrix of the world after the Mediator.... Through you we hold the certain pledges of our Redemption; through you we hope to reach the heavenly Kingdom.... Through you all glory, honor and holiness vouchsafed to the human race from the first Adam to the last ages has been granted, is being granted, will be granted to apostles, prophets, martyrs and all the just and humble of heart—O you only Stainless

One—and in you O Full-of-grace all creation exults with joy.
—*St. Ephraem of Edessa*
Doctor of the Church (+c. 373)

32. I salute you, O great Mediatress of peace between men and God.

—*St. Ephraem of Edessa*
Doctor of the Church (+c. 373)

33. This great Virgin and Mother found grace to restore thereby salvation to all men.
—*St. Peter Chrysologus, Bp. C.*
Doctor of the Church (+c. 450)

34. O Mary, God has decided on committing all good gifts that He has provided for men to your hands, and therefore He has entrusted all treasures and riches of grace to you.
—*St. Ildephonsus, Bp. C. (+667)*

35. While living among us, only a tiny bit of our earth did possess you. Now that you ascended on high the entire world will clasp you to its bosom as the universal peace-maker between it and the offended God.

—*St. Andrew of Crete (+720)*

36. No one, O you Most Pure One, receives God's gifts but through your hands. No one, O you Most Worthy of Honor, is given grace by the Divine Mercy but by you.
—*St. Germanus of Constantinople, Bp. C. (+c. 732)*

37. This most gentle dove winging her wondrous way to the fair fields of Heaven does not cease to protect us here on earth.

From Heaven's heights she put to flight the wicked angels, for she is there as our ever-active Mediatrix with God.

—*St. Theodore Studites* (+826)

38. In your hands, O Mary, are the riches of the Divine mercies. You alone are the one chosen to receive such a great grace.

—*St. Peter Damian, Bp. C.*
Doctor of the Church (+1072)

39. What all saints can do *with* you, you can do yourself and *without* them. . . . If you are silent, none can pray for me or help me; but if you do speak, all can pray for me, all can hasten to my aid.

—*St. Anselm, O.S.B., Bp. C.*
Doctor of the Church (+1109)

40. By you we have access to the Son, O blessed finder of grace, bearer of life and mother of salvation, that we may receive Him by you, Who through you was given to us.

—*St. Bernard of Clairvaux, Cist.*
Doctor of the Church (+1153)

41. Christ could suffice; for indeed, all our sufficiency is from Him; but we have need of an intercessor with Christ, nor is there anyone more influential than Mary.

—*St. Bernard of Clairvaux, Cist.*
Doctor of the Church (+1153)

42. No other created being can obtain for us so many and such eminent graces from God as His Mother.

—*St. William of Paris* (+1202)

43. The Virgin is called full of grace because she distributes this Divine life to all men.

—*St. Thomas Aquinas, O.P., C.*
Doctor of the Church (+1274)

44. The moon, set between the sun and the earth, gives to the earth the light she receives from the sun. Thus, Mary, Mediatrix between God and us, transmits to the earth the heavenly graces she receives from the Divine Sun.

—*St. Bonaventure, O.F.M., Bp. C.*
Doctor of the Church (+1274)

45. You are that most faithful dove of Noe who has most faithfully stood forth as Mediatrix between the Most High God and the world submerged in a spiritual deluge. The crow was unfaithful, the dove most faithful. Eve was the unfaithful mediatrix of perdition; Mary was the faithful Mediatrix of salvation. St. Bernard says: "Mary was the faithful Mediatrix, who prepared the antidote of salvation for both men and women."

—*St. Bonaventure, O.F.M., Bp. C.*
Doctor of the Church (+1274)

46. There are various types of "fullness" of grace. Among them is the fullness which receives solely for the purpose of giving, and that is the fullness of the canal. Now the Blessed Virgin has this fullness: for all graces without exception pass by her hands.

—*St. Albertus Magnus, O.P., Pr. C.*
Doctor of the Church (+1280)

47. She is the Universal Dispenser of all heavenly gifts.

—*St. Albertus Magnus, O.P., Pr. C.*
Doctor of the Church (+1280)

48. O you Mother of All Graces, I think neither my soul nor any other sinful soul requires permission or a passport to repair to you. Are you not the immediate Mediatrix of all sinners?

—*Blessed Henry Suso, O.P.* (+1365)

49. Every good, every help, every grace that men have received and will receive from God until the end of time, came, and will come, to them by the intercession and through the hands of Mary.... When we find Mary, we find all.

—*Blessed Raymond Jordano, Ab.* (+1381)

50. Although Christ is our Head, from which every movement of Divine Grace flows into His Mystical Body, yet the Blessed Virgin is the neck through which the flood passes to the members of the Body, as Solomon testifies in saying of Christ (Cant. 6): *Your neck* (which is the Blessed Virgin) *is like a tower of ivory.* Wherefore St. Bernard says: "No grace comes from Heaven to earth unless it passes through the hands of Mary." Rightly, therefore, can she be said to be full of grace from whom all graces pour forth on the Church Militant.

—*St. Bernardine of Siena, O.F.M.* (+1444)

51. As every mandate of grace that is sent by a king passes through the palace gates, so does every grace that comes from Heaven to the world pass through the hands of Mary (the Gate of Heaven).

—*St. Bernardine of Siena, O.F.M.* (+1444)

52. Every grace granted to man has three degrees in order; for by God it is communicated to Christ, from Christ it passes to the Virgin, and from the Virgin it descends to us.

—*St. Bernardine of Siena, O.F.M.* (+1444)

53. From the time that the Virgin Mother conceived the Divine

Word, she obtained a kind of jurisdiction, so to say, over all the temporal manifestations of the Holy Ghost; so that no creature can acquire any grace from God that is not dispensed by this tender and compassionate Mother.

—*St. Bernardine of Siena, O.F.M.* (+1444)

54. "Full of grace." That was the Angel's salutation. How then can she who became the Mother of God be anything but the ladder of Paradise, the gate of Heaven, the advocate of the world, the terror of demons, the hope of sinners and the true and real Mediatrix between God and man?

—*St. Laurence Justinian* (+1455)

55. All graces that have ever been bestowed on men, all came through Mary.

—*St. Antoninus, O.P., Bp. C.* (+1459)

56. Observe that St. Elizabeth receives the Holy Ghost through the intervention of the Blessed Virgin, in order to teach us that we must make use of her as our Mediatrix with her Divine Son, if we wish to obtain the Holy Ghost. True, we could go direct to God and ask Him for His grace without the help of the Blessed Virgin and the Saints, but God has not so willed it.

—*St. Francis de Sales, Bp. C.*
Doctor of the Church (+1622)

57. Our Adorable Redeemer laid up in the Heart of His Mother the riches He acquired and all the eternal blessings He won for us during the thirty-three years of His sojourn in this world. "The Savior," says St. Bernard, "with both hands poured, in measure good and overflowing, all His treasures into her bosom." He wished her to be the treasury of His gifts and graces and He refuses to impart any grace except through her.

—*St. John Eudes, Pr. C.* (+1680)

58. She can impart those gifts of grace in many unusual ways which He alone understands Who has wished to endow her with His own prerogatives. All that we do understand is that His Divine Goodness never has given and never will give any grace to anybody but through the hands and the Heart of her who is the Treasurer and Almoner of all His gifts.

—St. John Eudes, Pr. C. (+1680)

59. God is the source of every good, and the absolute Master of all graces; Mary is only a pure creature, who receives whatever she obtains as a pure favor from God. But who can ever deny that it is most reasonable and proper to assert that God, in order to exalt this great creature, who more than all the others honored and loved Him during her life, and whom, moreover, He had chosen to be the Mother of His Son, our common Redeemer, wills that all graces that are granted to those whom He has redeemed should pass through and be dispensed by the hands of Mary? We most readily admit that Jesus Christ is the only Mediator of justice, and that by His merits He obtains for us all graces and salvation; but we say that Mary is the mediatress of grace; and that receiving all she obtains through Jesus Christ, and because she prays and asks for it in the Name of Jesus Christ, yet all the same whatever graces we receive, they come to us through her intercession.

—St. Alphonsus Liguori, C.SS.R., Bp. C.
Doctor of the Church (+1787)

60. The intercession of Mary is even necessary to salvation; we say necessary—not absolutely, but morally. This necessity proceeds from the will itself of God, that all graces that He dispenses should pass through the hands of Mary, according to the opinion of St. Bernard, and which we may now with safety call the general opinion of theologians and learned men. . . . It is maintained by Vega, Mendoza, Segneri, Paciucchelte,

Poire, Crasset and by numerous other learned authors.
                                      —*St. Alphonsus Liguori, C.SS.R., Bp. C.*
                                          Doctor of the Church (+1787)

61. She is called by the Venerable Abbot of Celles (Bl. Ray-
mond of Jordano, +1381) "the Treasure of God, and the
Treasure of graces"; by St. Peter Damian (+1072) "the Treasure of divine graces"; by Bl. Albert the Great (St. Albertus
Magnus, +1280) the "Treasurer of Jesus Christ"; by St.
Bernardine (+1444) "the Dispenser of graces"; by a learned
Greek, quoted by Petavius, "the storehouse of all good things."
. . . Richard of St. Laurence (+1245) says that "Mary is a
treasure, because God has placed all gifts of graces in her as
in a treasury, and thence He bestows great stipends on His
soldiers and laborers.
                                      —*St. Alphonsus Liguori, C.SS.R., Bp. C.*
                                          Doctor of the Church (+1787)

62. All the saints had great devotion to Our Lady. They realized
that no grace comes from heaven without passing through her
hands. We cannot enter a house without first speaking to the
porter, similarly, the Holy Virgin is the portress of Heaven
and we cannot gain entrance there without calling upon her aid.
                                      —*St. Jean-Baptiste-Marie Vianney,*
                                          Cure d'Ars (+1859)

63. God has entrusted Mary with the keeping, the adminis-
tration and distribution of all His graces, so that all His graces
and gifts pass through her hands; and, according to the power
she has received over them, as St. Bernard teaches, Mary gives
to whom she wills, the way she wills, when she wills and as
much as she wills, the graces of the Eternal Father, the virtues
of Jesus Christ and the gifts of the Holy Ghost.
                                      —*St. Louis-Marie Grignon de Montfort* (+1716)

XLVI

Prerogatives of Mary

1. Rejoice, O Virgin Mary, for you alone have destroyed all heresies throughout the world.

—*Officium B.V.M.*

2. The Holy Mother of God has been elevated above the choirs of angels in the heavenly kingdom.

—*A Versicle of the Magnificat on the Feast of the Assumption*

3. The Blood of Christ shed for our sake, and those members in which He offers to His Father the wounds He received, "the price of our liberty," are no other than the flesh and blood of the Virgin: since, as St. Augustine said, "the flesh and blood of Jesus is the flesh of Mary, and however much it was exalted in the glory of His resurrection, nevertheless the nature of His flesh derived from Mary remained and still remains the same" (*De Assumpt. B.V.M.*, c.v.).

—*Pope Leo XIII (+1903)*

4. God destined Mary as a bridge of salvation, by using which we might with safety pass over the stormy sea of this world, and reach the happy haven of paradise.

—*St. James of Nisibis (+c. 338)*

5. As by Mary heavenly peace was once for all given to the world, so by her are sinners still reconciled to God.

—*St. Epiphanius, Ab., Bp. C. (+403)*

6. Would you know how far this Virgin surpasses in dignity the Powers of Heaven? They with fear and trembling stand before God covering their faces with their wings; she offers up the human race to Him to Whom she gave birth. Through her we may obtain pardon for our sins. Hail, then, O Mother, heavenly being, Virgin-throne of God, the glory and the bulwark of the Church; pray for us constantly to Jesus your Son our Lord, that *through you* we may find mercy in the day of judgment, and attain to the good things laid up for those who love God.

—*St. John Chrysostom*
Doctor of the Church (+407)

7. Everywhere the holy Church of God sings, what it is unlawful to believe of any other of the saints, that the merits (of Mary) transcend those of all angels and archangels. This privilege—not, as it were, of nature, but of grace—belongs to the Virgin Mary.

—*St. Jerome, Pr. C.*
Doctor of the Church (+420)

8. Every gift, every grace, every good that we have and that we receive continually, we receive through Mary. If Mary did not exist, neither would we, nor would the world.

—*St. Laurence of Brindisi, O.F.M. Cap.*
Doctor of the Church (+1619)

9. God wants everyone, *everyone* to learn this truth from childhood on: that he who trusts in Mary, that he who relies on Mary will never be abandoned either in this world or in the next.

—*St. Laurence of Brindisi, O.F.M. Cap.*
Doctor of the Church (+1619)

10. Mary is the Queen of the true Faith.

—*St. Cyril of Alexandria, Bp. C.*
Doctor of the Church (+444)

11. She is the ladder of Heaven; for by Mary God descended from Heaven into the world, that by her men might ascend from earth to Heaven.

—*St. Fulgentius* (+533)

12. God excepted, she is higher than all.

—*St. Andrew of Crete* (+720)

13. There is an infinite difference between the Mother of God and the servants of God.

—*St. John Damascene, Pr. C.*
Doctor of the Church (+c. 749)

14. Mary is the light of all the faithful.

—*St. Methodius, C.* (+847)

15. The fourth mode in which God is in a creature is that of identity; this He is in the Blessed Virgin Mary, for He is one with her. Let every creature be silent and tremble, and scarcely dare glance at the immensity of so great a dignity.

—*St. Peter Damian, Bp. C.*
Doctor of the Church (+1072)

16. As the light of the moon and stars is entirely eclipsed on the appearance of the sun, that it is as if it were not, so also does Mary's glory so far exceed the splendor of all men and angels, that, so to say, they do not appear in Heaven.

—*St. Peter Damian, Bp. C.*
Doctor of the Church (+1072)

17. No one is equal to you, O Lady, for all are either above or beneath you: ABOVE MARY, GOD ONLY; BENEATH MARY, ALL THAT IS NOT GOD.

> —*St. Anselm, O.S.B., Bp. C.*
> *Doctor of the Church* (+1109)

18. This is the singular glory of our Virgin, that she merited to have her Son in common with God the Father.

> —*St. Bernard of Clairvaux, Cist.*
> *Doctor of the Church* (+1153)

19. *My abode is in the full assembly of saints* (Ecclus. 24:16). I (B.V.M.) hold in plenitude all that other saints have held in part.

> —*St. Bonaventure, O.F.M., Bp. C.*
> *Doctor of the Church* (+1274)

20. Mary is called the Gate of Heaven (*felix coeli porta*) because no one can enter that blessed Kingdom without passing through her.

> —*St. Bonaventure, O.F.M., Bp. C.*
> *Doctor of the Church* (+1274)

21. A privilege of Mary is that she alone above all creatures was in the body most familiar with God. For, what was never granted to any other creature, nor will ever be granted again in eternity—she bore God for nine months in her womb, she nourished God from her breasts full of heaven, for many years she sweetly brought up Our Lord, she had God subject to her, she handled and embraced her God in pure embraces and kisses with tender familiarity.

> —*St. Bonaventure, O.F.M., Bp. C.*
> *Doctor of the Church* (+1274)

22. *King Solomon also made a great throne of ivory* (3 Kings 10: 18). Mary is the throne of Solomon, great in grace and glory.

St. Bernard well says, "As much more grace than others as Mary obtained on earth, so great a degree of singular glory did she gain in Heaven."

—*St. Bonaventure, O.F.M., Bp. C.*
Doctor of the Church (+1274)

23. The Blessed Virgin, who was equal to and even more superior in merit to all men and angels, was exalted above all the celestial orders.

—*St. Thomas Aquinas. O.P., C.*
Doctor of the Church (+1274)

24. To be the Mother of God is the highest dignity after that of being God. Mary could not have been more closely united to God than she was without becoming God.

—*St. Albertus Magnus, O.P., Pr. C.*
Doctor of the Church (+1280)

25. I (Mary) am that dove of Noe (Gn. 8:2) which brought the olive-branch of peace to the Church.

—*St. Albertus Magnus, O.P., Pr. C.*
Doctor of the Church (+1280)

26. The Virgin Mary contemplates the majesty of God in incomparably closer proximity than all other creatures.

—*St. Albertus Magnus, O.P., Pr. C.*
Doctor of the Church (+1280)

27. She is the dispenser of Divine mercy.

—*St. Catherine of Siena, V.*
Doctor of the Church (+1380)

28. The prerogatives of all the saints, O Virgin, you have united in yourself.

—*Blessed Raymond Jordano, Ab.* (+1381)

29. The greatness and dignity of the Virgin are such, that God alone can comprehend it.

—*St. Bernardine of Siena, O.F.M. (+1444)*

30. To become Mother of God the Blessed Virgin had to be raised to a sort of equality with the Divine Persons by an almost infinity of graces.

—*St. Bernardine of Siena, O.F.M. (+1444)*

31. *And when the ark was lifted up, Moses said: Arise, O Lord, and let Your enemies be scattered* (Nm. 10:35). When Mary, the Ark of the New Testament, was raised to the dignity of Queen of Heaven, the power of hell over men was weakened and dissolved.

—*St. Bernardine of Siena, O.F.M. (+1444)*

32. *I will set My bow in the clouds, and it shall be the sign of a covenant between Me and between the earth* (Gn. 9:13). Mary is this bow of eternal peace; for, as God on seeing it remembers the peace promised to the earth, so does He, at the prayers of Mary, forgive the crimes of sinners and confirm His peace with them.

—*St. Bernardine of Siena, O.F.M. (+1444)*

33. How can she be otherwise than full of grace, who has been made the Ladder to Paradise, the Gate of Heaven, the most true Mediatress between God and man?

—*St. Laurence Justinian (+1455)*

34. It was sufficient to say of her, *Of whom was born, Jesus.* What more could you wish the Evangelists to have said of her greatness? Is it not enough that they declare that she was the Mother of God? In these few words, they recorded the greatest, the whole, of her precious gifts; and since the whole was therein

contained, it was unnecessary to enter into details.
—*St. Thomas of Villanova, O.S.A.* (+1555)

35. Be comforted, then, O you who fear; breathe freely and take courage, O wretched sinner; this great Virgin, who is the Mother of your God and Judge, is also the advocate of the whole human race; fit for this office, for she can do what she wills with God; most wise, for she knows all the means of appeasing Him; universal, for she welcomes all, and refuses to defend no one.
—*St. Thomas of Villanova, O.S.A.* (+1555)

36. Mary is not only the privileged Daughter of the Father, the beloved Spouse of the Holy Ghost, she is also the Mother of the Son of God. In this quality, she is united to Jesus in the eternal decrees and in the promises of the Savior made in the beginning of all time. It is by her that the head of the serpent is to be crushed (Gn. 3:13). She is united to her Divine Son in the oracles of the prophets. Isaias announces this branch of Jesse, and the blessed Fruit she is to bear (Is. 7:14); Jeremiah predicts this marvelous woman, Mother of a perfect Man (Jer. 31:22); David sings of this Queen seated on the right hand of the heavenly King (Ps. 44:10). The book of Wisdom describes the wonders of the temple that Wisdom had chosen for Its dwelling (Wis. 9, etc.). She is united to Jesus in the figures of the ancient law.... Eve was drawn from Adam's side; Mary draws all her merits from her Divine Son. Eve, seduced by an angel of darkness, was the first cause of our ruin; Mary, persuaded by an angel from Heaven, began the work of our Redemption. Her intercession and power are prefigured by Esther obtaining grace for her people, by Judith victorious over Holophernes; her Immaculate Conception by the burning bush which the flames surrounded without touching, by that wonderful fleece which alone in a vast plain received the dew of Heaven. She is united to the Son of God at the moment of the Incarnation. Then her Creator became

her Child (Ecclus. 24:12). The blood of Mary became the
Blood of Jesus, Jesus is flesh of her flesh; He lives with her
life, breathes with her breath; He is in her, to her, of her entirely. Thus the Angel says: *The Lord is with you* (Luke 1:28).
Elizabeth says: *Behold the Mother of my Lord* (v. 44). And the
Church, in the third General Council, declares: "If any one
refuse to call Mary Mother of God, let him be anathema" (*Acta
of the Council of Ephesus*). Best of all, the holy soul of Mary is
united to the adorable soul of Jesus. She conceived Him in
her Heart before receiving Him in her bosom, says St. Bernard.
She unites herself to Him by the most lively faith, the most
ardent charity, by the consent, the memory of which we revere
in the "Angelus," three times a day, and which associates her
with her whole destiny. So Mary is found with Jesus at Beth-
lehem, in Egypt, in Nazareth, in Jerusalem, and, above all,
on Calvary, where the sword of sorrow pierced her soul when
the lance opened the Heart of her Divine Son. Jesus ascends
to Heaven, and Mary is soon placed on His right hand, that
is, associated with His glory and His all-powerful action in
the salvation of the world; united to the King of Heaven in
an ineffable union. Here on earth the Son and the Mother
are united in the praises of the Fathers, in the prayers of the
Christian Liturgy, in the definitions of the councils, in the
solemnities of the Church. We see Christians honoring, always
in union, the Incarnation of Jesus, the Conception of Mary;
the Nativity of Jesus, the Nativity of Mary; the Presentation
of Jesus, the Presentation of Mary; the Baptism of Jesus, the
Purification of Mary; the Passion of Jesus, the Dolors of Mary;
the Ascension of Jesus, the Assumption of Mary; the Sacred
Heart of Jesus, the Holy Heart of Mary. (One could extend
these parallel honorings—the feasts of the Holy Name of Jesus,
the Holy Name of Mary; the feasts of the Good Shepherd,
of the Mother of the Divine Shepherd; the feasts of Christ
the King, of Our Lady Queen of Angels; the devotions to the
Prince of Peace, to Mary Queen of Peace; to the Holy Redeemer, to Mary Co-redemptrix; to the Divine Mediator,
to Mary Mediatrix; to the Divine Infant, to Maria Santissima

Bambina, etc., etc.). The Names of Jesus and Mary live always in the hearts and songs of the Faithful; their temples and their altars are always near together, and nothing is more inseparable in Christians' pious remembrance, their confidence, their invocation, their love, than JESUS and MARY.

—*St. Ignatius Loyola, Founder of the Company (Society) of Jesus* (+1556)

37. Mary is in all things similar to Christ, in nature, grace and glory: in nature, being of the same nature with Christ; in grace, being also holy and full of grace and the Holy Spirit; and in glory, being like Christ as the moon is like the sun and a queen is like the king. Yes, Mary resembles Christ in her predestination, her birth, her resurrection, her assumption, her glorification.

—*St. Laurence of Brindisi, O.F.M. Cap. Doctor of the Church* (+1619)

38. In Heaven the Mother of Fair Love is after Christ God's greatest blessing to the universal Church—the blessing of blessings, than which none greater could be thought out, since she does all things for us with God the Almighty.

—*St. Laurence of Brindisi, O.F.M. Cap. Doctor of the Church* (+1619)

39. Her dignity infinitely exceeds that of the angels, *having become so much superior to the angels as (she) has inherited a more excellent name than they* (Heb. 1:4). For the dignity of the angels and saints compared to that of the Mother of God is as the moon compared to the brilliance of the sun. Hence, Mary, as we read in the Apocalypse (1:12), is clothed with the sun, crowned with the stars, and has the moon beneath her feet.

—*St. Laurence of Brindisi, O.F.M. Cap. Doctor of the Church* (+1619)

40. Nothing under God can be more glorious than Mary. She is Queen of Heaven, Queen of Angels, Empress of Paradise, Daughter of the Heavenly Father, Mother of the Only-begotten Son of God, Spouse of the Holy Spirit. *In her dwells the fullness of the Godhead bodily* (Col. 2:9).

—St. Laurence of Brindisi, O.F.M. Cap.
Doctor of the Church (+1619)

XLVII

Absolute Confidence in Mary

1. Who, ever, O Lady, faithfully employed your all-powerful aid and was abandoned by you?

—Pope St. Eutychian (+c. 283)

2. Who is there that ever had recourse to her and was not relieved?

—Pope Innocent III (+1216)

3. You know, Venerable Brethren, that all our confidence is in the Most Holy Virgin, for God has conferred upon her the fullness of all perfection; let us hold it for certain that every hope the world has, every grace, every means of salvation, comes from her.... Such is the will of Him Who has willed us to have all through Mary.

—Pope Pius IX (+1878)

4. Let Christians run to Mary with confidence in all their temptations and in all their needs: for no one has anything to fear, no one can despair of the success of any enterprise with her for guide, for patron, for shield, for protectress. She loves

us with a mother's love. She takes upon herself the burden of our salvation.

—*Pope Pius IX* (+1878)

5.   While nature itself made the name of mother the sweetest of all names, and has made motherhood the very model of tender and foresighted love, no tongue is eloquent to put in words what every devout soul feels, namely, how intense is the flame of affectionate and active charity which burns in Mary, in her who is truly our Mother not in a human way but through Christ.... Accordingly, let us approach Mary boldly, wholeheartedly beseeching her by the bonds of her motherhood which unite her so closely to Jesus and at the same time to us; let us with deepest devotion invoke her constant aid in the prayer (Rosary) which she herself has indicated and which is most acceptable to her; then with good reason shall we rest with an easy and joyous mind under the protection of this best of mothers.

—*Pope Leo XIII* (+1903)

6.   God could create an infinity of suns, one more brilliant than the other; an infinity of worlds, one more marvelous than the other; an infinity of angels, one more holy than the other. But a creature more holy, more ravishing, more gracious than His Mother He could not make: for in making her His Mother, He gave her at once, so to say, all that He could give of beauty and goodness and holiness and sanctity in the treasury of His omnipotence.

—*St. Leonard of Port Maurice, O.F.M.* (+1751)

7.   You, O Lord, have given us in Mary arms that no force of war can overcome, and a trophy never to be destroyed.

—*St. James of Nisibis* (+c. 338)

8.   Look down upon us, O most compassionate Mother; cast your eyes of mercy on us, for we are your servants, and

in you have we placed all our confidence.

—*St. Euthymius the Great* (+473)

9.   While I keep my hope in you unconquerable, O Mother of God, I shall be safe. I will fight and overcome my enemies with no other buckler than your protection and your all-powerful aid.

—*St. John Damascene, Pr. C.*
Doctor of the Church (+c. 749)

10. O blessed confidence, O safe refuge, Mother of God and our Mother!

—*St. Anselm, O.S.B., Bp. C.*
Doctor of the Church (+1109)

11. The Mother of God is my Mother. How firm, then, should be our confidence, since our salvation depends on the judgment of a good Brother and a tender Mother.

—*St. Anselm, O.S.B., Bp. C.*
Doctor of the Church (+1109)

12. Turn not away your eyes from the splendor of this star, if you will not be overwhelmed by storms. If the winds of temptation arise, if you strike on the rocks of temptation, or tribulation, look upon the star, call on Mary. . . . Following her, you stray not; praying to her, you shall never despair; thinking of her, you shall never err; if she upholds you, you shall not fall; under her protection you shall not fear; if she is your guide, you shall not grow weary; with her favor you shall attain your end; and so in yourself you shall experience how truly it is said: *And the name of the Virgin was Mary.*

—*St. Bernard of Clairvaux, Cist.*
Doctor of the Church (+1153)

13. After God, it is our greatest glory, O Mary, to behold you, to adhere to you, to abide in the defense of your protection.
— *St. Bernard of Clairvaux, Cist.*
Doctor of the Church (+1153)

14. You, O Queen elect, are the gate of all grace, the door of compassion that never yet was shut. Heaven and earth may pass away, ere you will permit anyone who earnestly seeks your assistance to depart from you without obtaining it. Behold, for this very reason are you the first object of my soul when I awake, the last when I lie down to sleep. How should anything which your pure hands present before God and commend to Him, how small soever in itself, be rejected?
— *Blessed Henry Suso, O.P.* (+1365)

15. You are our only refuge, help and asylum.
— *St. Thomas of Villanova, O.S.A.* (+1555)

16. "Who," says Cardinal Bellarmine (St. Robert Bellarmine, Doctor of the Church, +1621: *De Sept. Verb.* 1, i, c. 12), "would ever dare to snatch these children from the bosom of Mary, when they have taken refuge there? What power of hell, or what temptation, can overcome them, if they place their confidence in the patronage of this great Mother, the Mother of God and our Mother?"
— *St. Alphonsus Liguori, C.SS.R., Bp. C.*
Doctor of the Church (+1787)

17. You will do well in having special recourse to the glorious Virgin Mary, for she is the one among all pure creatures who most signalled herself in the virtue of humility.
— *St. Aloysius Gonzaga, S.J.* (+1591)

XLVIII

True Devotion to Mary

1.   After having laid bare and condemned the false devotions
to the most Holy Virgin (the critical devotees, the scrupulous,
the external, the presumptuous, the inconstant and the self-
interested), we must in a few words characterize the true devotion. It must be: 1) interior; 2) tender; 3) holy; 4) constant;
and 5) disinterested.

    1) True devotion to Our Lady is interior; that is, it comes
from the mind and the heart. It flows from the esteem we
have for her, the high idea we have formed of her greatness,
and the love which we have for her.

    2) It is tender; that is, full of confidence in her, like a
child's confidence in his loving mother. This confidence makes
the soul have recourse to her in all its bodily and mental necessities, with much simplicity, trust and tenderness. It implores
the aid of its good Mother at all times, in all places and about
all things: in its doubts, that it may be enlightened; in its
wanderings, that it may be brought into the right path; in
its temptations, that it may be supported; in its weaknesses,
that it may be strengthened; in its falls, that it may be lifted up;
in its discouragements, that it may be cheered; in its scruples,
that they may be taken away; in the crosses, toils and dis-
appointments of life, that it may be consoled under them.
In a word, in all the evils of body and mind, the soul ordinarily
has recourse to Mary, without fear of annoying her or displeas-
ing Jesus Christ.

    3) True devotion to Our Lady is holy; that is to say, it leads
the soul to avoid sin, and to imitate the virtues of the Blessed
Virgin, particularly her profound humility, her lively faith, her
blind obedience, her continual prayer, her universal mortifica-

tion, her divine purity, her ardent charity, her heroic patience, her angelic sweetness and her divine wisdom. These are the ten principal virtues of the Most Holy Virgin.

4) True devotion to Our Lady is constant. It confirms the soul in good, and does not let it easily abandon its spiritual exercises. It makes it courageous in opposing the world in its fashions and maxims, the flesh in its weariness and passions and the devil in his temptations; so that a person truly devout to Our Blessed Lady is not changeable, irritable, scrupulous nor timid. It is not that such a person does not fall, or change sometimes in the sensible feeling of devotion. But when he falls, he rises again by stretching out his hand to his good Mother. When he loses the taste and relish of devotion, he does not become disturbed because of that, for the just and faithful client of Mary lives on the faith (Heb. 10:38) of Jesus and Mary, and not the sentiments and sensibilities.

5) Lastly, true devotion to Our Lady is disinterested; that is to say, it inspires the soul not to seek itself but God only, and God in His Holy Mother. A true client of Mary does not serve that august Queen from a spirit of lucre and interest, nor for his own good, whether temporal or eternal, corporal or spiritual, but *exclusively because she deserves to be served and God alone in her*. He does not love Mary just because she obtains favors for him, or because he hopes she will, but *solely because she is so worthy of love*. It is on this account that he loves and serves her as faithfully in his disgusts and drynesses as in his sweetnesses and sensible fervors. He loves her as much on Calvary as at the marriage of Cana. Oh, how agreeable and precious in the eyes of God and of His Holy Mother is such a client of Our Blessed Lady, who has no self-seeking in his service of her! But in these days how rare is such a gift.

—*St. Louis-Marie Grignon de Montfort* (+1716)

XLIX

The Holy Slavery

1.   *Put your feet into her fetters, and your neck into her chains . . . .*
Then shall her fetters be a strong defense for you, and a firm founda-
tion, and her chain a robe of glory.

—*(Ecclus. 6:25, 30)*

2.   *They that serve her shall be servants to the Holy One: and God*
loves them that love her.

—*(Ecclus. 4:15)*

3.   I desire to be the servant of the Son; but because no one will
ever be so without serving the Mother, for this reason I desire
servitude to Mary.

—*St. Ildephonsus, Bp. C.* (+667)

4.   Govern me, O my Queen, and leave me not to myself.

—*St. Bonaventure, O.F.M., Bp. C.*
Doctor of the Church (+1274)

5.   Even should she take my life, I would still hope in her and,
full of confidence, would desire to die before her image.

—*St. Bonaventure, O.F.M., Bp. C.*
Doctor of the Church (+1274)

6.   Command me; employ me as you will, and chastise me
when I do not obey; for the chastisements that come from your
hands will be to me pledges of salvation. I would rather be your
servant than the ruler of the earth. *I am yours; save me* (Ps. 118:

94). Accept me, O Mary, for your own, and as yours, take charge of my salvation.

—*St. Alphonsus Liguori, C.SS.R., Bp. C.*
Doctor of the Church (+1787)

7. Those who undertake this holy slavery should have a special devotion to the great mystery of the Incarnation of the Word on 25 March. Indeed, the Incarnation is the mystery proper of this practice, inasmuch as it is a devotion inspired by the Holy Ghost: first, to honor and imitate the ineffable dependence which God the Son has been pleased to have on Mary, for His Father's glory and our salvation—which dependence particularly appears in this mystery, where Jesus is a captive and a slave in the bosom of the Divine Mother, and depends on her for all things; secondly, to thank God for the incomparable graces He has given Mary, and particularly for having chosen her to be His most Holy Mother, which choice was made in this mystery. These are the two principal ends of the slavery of Jesus in Mary.

Have the goodness to observe that I say generally, "the slave of Jesus in Mary," "the slavery of Jesus in Mary." I might in good truth, as many have done before (e.g. Boudon: *Le Saint Esclavage de la Mere de Dieu*), say the "slave of Mary," "the slavery of the Holy Virgin," but . . . it is better for us to say "the slavery of Jesus in Mary," and call ourselves the slaves of Jesus Christ rather than the slaves of Mary, taking the denomination of our devotion rather from its Last End, which is Jesus Christ, than from the road and the means to the end, which is Mary. Though I repeat that in truth we may do either, as I have done myself. . . . The principal mystery we celebrate and honor in the devotion is the mystery of the Incarnation, wherein we can see Jesus only in Mary, and incarnate in her bosom. Hence it is more to the purpose to speak of the slavery of Jesus in Mary, and of Jesus residing and reigning in Mary, according to that beautiful prayer of so many great men: "O Jesus, living in Mary: come and live in your servants," etc. (see Section XXXI, 11).

This manner of speaking sets forth still more the intimate union between Jesus and Mary. They are so intimately united that the one is altogether in the other. Jesus is altogether in Mary and Mary is altogether in Jesus, or, rather, she exists no more, but Jesus alone is all in her, and it were easier to separate the light from the sun than Mary from Jesus; so that we might call Our Lord, Jesus of Mary, and our Blessed Lady, Mary of Jesus.

—*St. Louis-Marie Grignon de Montfort* (+1716)

8.   A person who is thus voluntarily consecrated and sacrificed to Jesus Christ through Mary can no longer dispose of the value of any of his good actions. All he suffers, all he thinks, all the good he says or does, belongs to Mary, in order that she may dispose of it according to the will of her Son and His greatest glory—without, however, that dependence interfering in any way with the obligations of the state we may be in at present, or may be placed in for the future; for example, without interfering with the obligations of a priest who, by his office or otherwise, ought to apply the satisfactory and impetratory value of the Holy Mass to some private person. For we make the offering of this devotion according to the order of God and the duties of our state.

—*St. Louis-Marie Grignon de Montfort* (+1716)

9.   If we can conceive on earth no employment more lofty than the service of God—if the last servant of God is richer, more powerful and more noble than all the kings and emperors of this earth, unless they are also the servants of God—what must be the riches, the power and the dignity of the faithful and perfect servant of God, who is devoted to His service entirely and without reserve, to the utmost possible extent? Such is the faithful and loving slave of Jesus in Mary who has given himself up entirely to the service of that King of kings, by the hands of His Holy Mother, and has reserved nothing for himself. Not all the gold of earth nor all beauties of the heavens can repay him. ... This devotion (of the holy slavery) makes us give to Jesus and Mary, without reserve, all our thoughts, words, actions and

sufferings, all the moments of our life, in such sort that, whether we wake or sleep, whether we eat or drink, whether we do great actions or very little ones, it is always true to say that, whatever we do, even without thinking of it, is by virtue of our offering at least, if it has not been intentionally retracted, done for Jesus and Mary. What a consolation this is! Moreover, there is no other practice equal to this for enabling us to rid ourselves easily of a certain proprietorship which imperceptibly creeps into our best actions. Our good Jesus gives us this great grace in recompense for the heroic and disinterested action of giving over to Him, by the hands of His Holy Mother, all the value of our good works. If He gives a hundredfold even in this world to those who, for His love, quit outward and temporal and perishable goods (Mt. 19:29), what will that hundredfold be which He will give to the man who sacrifices for Him even his inward and spiritual goods!... The most Holy Virgin, who is a Mother of sweetness and mercy, and who never lets herself be outdone in love and liberality, seeing that we give ourselves entirely to her, to honor and to serve her, and for that end strip ourselves of all that is dearest to us, in order to adorn her, meets us in the same spirit. She also gives her whole self, and gives in an unspeakable manner, to him who gives all to her. She causes him to be engulfed in the abyss of her graces. She adorns him with her merits; she supports him with her power; she illuminates him with her light; she inflames him with her love; she communicates to him her virtues: her humility, her faith, her piety and the rest. She makes herself his bail, his supplement, and his dear everything toward Jesus. In a word, as that consecrated person is all Mary's, so Mary is all his; after such a fashion that we can say of that perfect servant and child of Mary what St. John Evangelist said of himself, that he took the Holy Virgin for all his goods: *The disciple took her for his own* (John 19: 27).... Oh, how happy is the man who has given everything to Mary, and has entrusted himself to Mary, and lost himself in her, in everything and for everything. He belongs to Mary, and Mary belongs all to him.

—*St. Louis-Marie Grignon de Montfort* (+1716)

L

Entire Consecration to Jesus Through Mary

1.   All our perfection consists in being conformed, united and consecrated to Jesus Christ: and therefore the most perfect of all devotions is, without any doubt, that which most perfectly conforms, unites and consecrates us to Jesus Christ. Now, Mary being the most conformed of all creatures to Jesus Christ, that which most consecrates and conforms the soul to Our Lord is devotion to His Holy Mother, and the more a soul is consecrated to Mary, the more it is consecrated to Jesus. Hence it comes to pass that the most perfect consecration to Jesus Christ is nothing else than a perfect and entire consecration of ourselves to the Blessed Virgin, and this is the devotion which I teach; or, in other words, a perfect renewal of the vows and promises of Baptism. This devotion consists, then, in giving ourselves entirely to Our Lady, in order to belong entirely to Jesus through her. We must give her 1) our body, with all its senses and its members; 2) our soul, with all its powers; 3) our exterior goods of fortune, whether present or to come; 4) our interior and spiritual goods, which are our merits and our virtues, and our good works, past, present and future. In a word, we must give her all we have in the order of nature and in the order of grace, and all that may become ours in the future, in the orders of nature, grace and glory; and this we must do without the reserve of so much as one farthing, one hair, or one least good action; and we must do it also for all eternity; and we must do it, further, without pretending to, or hoping for, any other recompense for our offering and service except the honor of belonging to Jesus Christ through Mary and in Mary—even though that sweet Mistress were not, as she always is, the most generous and the most grateful of creatures. . . . In this conse-

cration of ourselves to Our Lady, we give her all the satisfactory, impetratory and meritorious value of our actions; in other words, the satisfactions and the merits of all our good works. We give her all our merits, graces and virtues—not to com-municate them to others, for our merits, graces and virtues are, properly speaking, incommunicable, and it is only Jesus Christ Who, in making Himself our surety with His Father, is able to communicate His merits—but we give her them to keep them, augment them and embellish them for us. Our satisfactions, however, we give her, to communicate to whom she likes, and for the greatest glory of God. It follows from this, that by this devotion, we give to Jesus Christ in the most perfect manner, inasmuch as it is by Mary's hands, all we can give Him, and far more than by any other devotions in which we give Him either a part of our time, or a part of our good works, or a part of our satisfactions and mortifications; because here everything is given and consecrated to Him, even the right of disposing of our interior goods, and of the satisfactions which we gain by our good works day after day.... We consecrate ourselves at one and the same time to the most Holy Virgin and to Jesus Christ: to the most Holy Virgin as to the perfect means which Jesus Christ has chosen whereby to unite Himself to us, and us to Him; and to Our Lord as to our last end, to Whom as our Redeemer and our God we owe all we are.

I have said that this devotion may most justly be called a perfect renewal of the vows or promises of Holy Baptism.... Men, says St. Thomas, make a vow at their Baptism to renounce the devil and all his pomps (Summa Theol., 2 a 2 ae, q. 88, art. 2, arg. I). This vow, says St. Augustine, is the greatest and most indispensable of all vows (Epistola 59 ad Paulinum). It is thus also that canonists speak: "The principal vow is the one we make at Baptism.".... The Council of Sens, convoked by order of Louis the Debonair to remedy the disorders of Christians, which were then so great, judged that the principal cause of that corruption of morals arose from the oblivion and the ignorance in which men lived of the obligations of Holy Baptism; and it could think of no better means for remedying so great an evil than to persuade Christians to renew the vows and promises of Baptism. The Catechism of the Council of Trent, the faithful interpreter of that holy Council, exhorts the parish priests to do the same thing, and to induce the people to remind themselves, and to believe, that they are bound and consecrated as slaves to Our Lord Jesus Christ, their Redeemer and their Lord. These are its words: "The parish priest shall exhort the faithful people so that they may know that it is most just. . .that we should devote and consecrate ourselves forever to our Redeemer and Lord as His very slaves (*Catech. Conc. Trid.*, Pt. 1a, cap. 3, art. 2, n. 15, *De secundo Symboli articulo, in finem*). Now, if the Councils, the Fathers and even experience shows us that the best means of remedying the irregularities of Christians is by making them call to mind the obligations of their Baptism, and persuading them to renew no w the vows they made then, is it not only right that we should do it in perfect manner, by this devotion and consecration of ourselves to Our Lord through His Holy Mother? I say in a perfect manner: because in this consecrating of ourselves to Him, we make use of the most perfect of all means, namely, the Blessed Virgin.

—*St. Louis-Marie Grignon de Montfort* (+1716)

2.   O Mary, I give you my heart. Grant me to be always yours. Jesus and Mary, be ever my friends; and, for love of you, grant me to die a thousand deaths rather than to have the misfortune of committing a single mortal sin.

—*St. Dominic Savio* (+1857)

21 Ecumenical Councils of the Church

An ecumenical council is an assembly of the college of bishops with and under the presidency of the pope, which has supreme authority over the Church in matters pertaining to faith, morals, worship, and discipline.

1. Nicea (325)
2. Constantinople I (381)
3. Ephesus (431)
4. Chalcedon (451)
5. Constantinople II (553)
6. Constantinople III (680-681)
7. Nicea II (787)
8. Constantinople IV (869-870)

9. Lateran I (1123)
10. Lateran II (1139)
11. Lateran III (1179)
12. Lateran IV (1215)
13. Lyons I (1245)
14. Lyons II (1274)
15. Vienne (1311-1312)
16. Constance (1414-1418)
17. Florence (1438-1445)
18. Lateran V (1512-1517)
19. Trent (1545-1563)
20. Vatican I (1869-1870)
21. Vatican II (1962-1965)

Doctors of the Church

The qualifications required to be made a Doctor of the Church are: outstanding wisdom, outstanding holiness, and proclamation by the Church. There are Doctors from both Eastern and Western Churches. All Doctors not designated Eastern are Doctors of the Western Church.

St. Athanasius (+373)	(Eastern)
St. Basil (+379)	(Eastern)
St. Cyril of Jerusalem (+386)	(Eastern)
St. Gregory Nazianzen (+389)	(Eastern)
St. John Chrysostom (+407)	(Eastern)
St. Hilary (+368)	
St. Ephraem (+373)	(Eastern)
St. Ambrose (+379)	
St. Jerome (+420)	
St. Augustine (+430)	
St. Cyril of Alexandria (+440)	(Eastern)
St. Peter Chrysologos (+450)	
St. Leo the Great (+461)	
St. Gregory the Great (+604)	
St. Isidore of Seville (+636)	
St. Bede the Venerable (+735)	
St. John Damascene (+749)	(Eastern)
St. Peter Damian (+1072)	
St. Anselm (+1109)	
St. Bernard (+1153)	
St. Anthony of Padua (+1231)	
St. Thomas Aquinas (+1274)	
St. Bonaventure (+1274)	
St. Albert the Great (+1280)	
St. Catherine of Siena (+1380)	
St. Teresa of Avila (+1582)	
St. John of the Cross (+1591)	
St. Peter Canisius (+1597)	
St. Laurence of Brindisi (+1619)	
St. Robert Bellarmine (+1621)	
St. Francis de Sales (+1622)	
St. Alphonsus de Liguori (+1787)